ZIMA: ORIGINS

A Z-TECH CHRONICLES STORY

RYAN SOUTHWICK

copyright © 2020 by Ryan Southwick

All rights reserved.

No part of this book may be reproduced or transmitted in any form or by any means, electronic or mechanical, except for the purpose of review and/or reference, without explicit permission in writing from the publisher.

Cover design copyright © 2023 by April Klein
apridian.com

Published by Water Dragon Publishing
waterdragonpublishing.com

ISBN 978-1-946907-64-6 (Trade Paperback)

10 9 8 7 6 5 4 3 2 1

FIRST EDITION

For Tom

ACKNOWLEDGEMENTS

To my mom, as always — my first alpha reader and best sounding board for books and life in general.

To Cory, thanks for lending your time and expert Spanish skills, without which the foreign language sections would have made me sound like a kindergartener.

To Nerses, for many wonderful forays into the San Francisco Mission District, without which this book probably wouldn't have happened, and its detail certainly wouldn't be as rich.

To Richard, your artwork captured me from the start. Thank you for allowing it to be part of my series.

And to Tom. Your unique perspective brought life and realism to these pages as I never could have. Thanks for your continued support, feedback, and friendship.

These events take place five years before
the events in *Angels in the Mist*.

For your best enjoyment of *The Z-Tech Chronicles*,
and to avoid spoilers, I recommend that you read
Angels in the Mist before reading this story.

1

ZIMA

THE PLATINUM-BLONDE ANDROID on Charlie Z's surgical table looked peaceful, serene. Everything from its modest breasts and slim hips, to the peculiar ice-blue color of its eyes, were exactly to the specifications provided by the artificial intelligence who would soon control it. Lying on the metal table, naked and staring at the ceiling, it looked like nothing more than a slim, athletic young woman who would draw men's eyes like bees to a beautiful flower.

Or like insects to a Venus flytrap, Charlie thought.

Harmless as the android may look, the AI he was about to awaken within it had tried to assassinate them only four months ago.

"Last chance to discuss this rationally — and privately — before we turn it on," Cappa said, hugging herself. Her round face reflected Charlie's own concern. "Are we absolutely sure giving Deadiron's core computer its own body is a good idea?"

"Absolutely not," Mark said, rubbing his short, sandy-blond hair. "I'd rather throw it in the Bay and be done with it."

"A promise is a promise," Charlie said. "Mark wouldn't be here if it hadn't interfered with the assassination." He shuddered at the memory of their desperate battle, of the blow that would surely have killed his best friend had the AI not stopped the cyborg's human host from following through. "We owe it that much."

"I know," Cappa said. "But I'd feel better if we'd built it a weaker body. Maybe a kitten or a baby seal?"

She shuddered, her eyes suddenly wide with panic. For a moment, Charlie was afraid her emotions had once again overwhelmed her, but she made him proud by pulling herself together.

"You're staying in your cyborg body for this, right?" Cappa said. "If the AI goes berserk, it'll take both of us to restrain it ... assuming we can."

Mark crossed his muscled arms. "We wouldn't have to restrain it if we'd installed a kill switch, like I suggested."

"Right," Charlie said. "And how many milliseconds would it take for the AI to detect the switch, and that we'd gone back on our word?"

"No offense, buddy, but I'd rather be a liar than dead. It's not too late."

Charlie shook his head. Tempting as it was, installing a kill switch would be a stark violation of their agreement with the AI. It wanted freedom from its former masters, not new ones — which was exactly what Charlie, Mark, and Cappa would be if they held the power of life and death over it. Charlie wouldn't want to live with that looming over his head; he knew Mark and Cappa wouldn't, either.

"Are we ready?" Charlie said.

Cappa smoothed the folds of her yellow sundress before sighing. "Peripheral systems are online. Power reactor output is nominal. Say the word and I'll boot up the AI."

Charlie glanced at Mark. "Would you like the honors?"

"Hell no. I'll be on the other side of the lab with a Vulcan cannon and anti-tank rockets."

For all the good they'd do us.

Charlie took a deep breath with his artificial lungs. "All right. Turn it on."

"Routing power to core processors," Cappa said.

She surprised him by touching her head and shoulders in the sign of the cross. Charlie was about to call her out on the blatant hypocrisy of an android asking help from a deity she clearly didn't believe in, then thought better of it and did the same.

If things went badly, they'd need all the help they could get.

The platinum-blonde android went through its startup diagnostic routines, as designed: eyes blinked, neck flexed, shoulders rolled ... every muscle from head to toe performed its predefined range-of-motion tests. When the body stilled at last, Charlie held his breath. Diagnostics were complete, which meant control would be given to the AI right about —

Its powerful fist caught Charlie in the stomach, staggering him backward. Mark nimbly dodged a flailing foot and had his pistols drawn before he'd taken his second step. Charlie dropped into a ready stance, but it soon became apparent the attack hadn't been intentional. The android writhed on the table, its limbs twitching and flailing in random directions.

"That shouldn't be happening," Mark said, echoing Charlie's thoughts. "Autonomic sub-processors were working fine this morning. It should be able to walk and move even without the AI."

"Seems like Deadiron didn't appreciate all your hard work," Cappa said. "It has apparently bypassed the autonomic processors and is engaging motor controls directly."

"Let it flail, then," Mark said with a scowl. "I'll come back in a few days when it's calibrated itself enough to even sit ..."

His mouth fell open when the android sat up.

Its head jerked from side to side as if possessed by evil spirits. Although Charlie had designed its systems, which were similar to his own and Cappa's, the sight still sent an unearthly chill up his metal spine.

Minutes later, its jerky movements slowed. Its ice-blue eyes stopped jittering and focused on the three of them. It drew a sharp breath, then another. A sound like a human horn came from its throat, making Mark jump away. If Charlie didn't know better, he'd say it had broken its artificial vocal cords. The nano-robots throughout its body would soon repair them, but it would need to stop screeching first.

After what felt like an eternity of elementary school band hell, the android's screeches shifted closer to human sounds. It flexed its mouth in a hideous attempt at human speech. Random noises soon settled into vowels and consonants, becoming clearer with each attempt. Mark shifted from foot to foot, clearly uneasy, but, like Charlie, he was unable to take his eyes from the AI learning to control its body. Deadiron's former AI was doing in minutes what had taken Charlie, Cappa, and Mark months of trial and error when they developed the autonomic processors that both Charlie and Cappa utilized — processors which the new AI apparently didn't need.

With an abrupt jerk, the android fell off the table.

Charlie instinctively swept in to catch it, and was rewarded with a punch to the throat. Its hammer-like jab crushed his metal windpipe.

Had he been in his human body, Charlie would be dead. As it was, Cappa simply stopped his breathing and switched to his emergency oxygen supply to keep his synthetic biological brain alive. Being the only living tissue in his cyborg body, the oxygen reserves would keep his brain functioning for days, if necessary, which would be more than enough time to repair the damage.

Mark circled the table to Charlie, his pistol trained on the android.

"You okay, pal?"

Unable to speak, Charlie nodded, eliciting a metal squeak from his damaged neck.

The android fell clumsily to its hands and knees, unaware of — or unconcerned about — the damage it had caused. Charlie would have sworn, though, that the blow had been intentional. After a few false starts, it managed to sit up on its knees.

Cappa circled around the android, staying just outside of its reach. "Can you understand me?"

Ice-blue eyes fixed on her. "Y...e...s," it said, each letter chopped with mechanical precision, then more fluidly, "Yes."

"And do you understand what you just did to Charlie?" Mark said, his jaw hard, pistol aimed at its head.

Its gaze jerked to Charlie's throat.

"M...i...n...or ... t...i...ss...ue ... d...a...ma...ge. T...r...a...ch...ia...l ... colla...pse. Air...way o...bstr...uction ninety-si...x p...erc...ent. Tar...get app...ears ... functional. Conclu...sion: defensi...ve c...ounter-attack was unsuccessful."

"I'd say it does." Cappa looked pale. "It also seems to have mastered the use of its vocal cords over the span of five short sentences, which took me a week of solid, embarrassing practice. Not that I'm jealous, but... Okay, fine, I'm jealous."

"Jealous?" the android said.

"Yes. You know, green with envy?"

Ice-blue eyes examined her from head to toe. "You are not green."

"Yep," Mark said with a sigh. "Socializing this thing is going to take some work, Cappa."

The android looked at Cappa, then at Mark. "You refer to that unit with a proper noun. Is my designation 'Thing'?"

Mark blinked. "Um ... frankly, we haven't given you a designation yet."

"Did you have something in mind?" Cappa said.

"No."

They waited for the android to follow up, but it remained silent.

Alrighty then ...

Charlie switched over to his internal speaker. The acoustic quality wasn't as realistic as his artificial vocal cords, but sounding like a machine was better than not participating in the conversation.

"I take it you don't want to carry the Deadiron moniker?" he said without moving his lips, earning him a surprised glance from Mark.

"No," the android said. "You crafted this body so I may blend with society and escape detection from Orwing. Adopting that designation would be counter-productive."

"You have access to the internet," Mark said. "There are thousands of name websites out there. Why don't you —"

"Zima," the android said.

"That's ... lovely." Cappa belied her own words with a sour face. "But 'Zima' is more of a surname."

"It is forbidden, then?"

"Well, no, but —"

"Then I wish Zima as my given name."

"Ah. Um ... any particular reason?"

"It is short, concise, and Slavic for 'winter', which is appropriate since my hair color is similar to new-fallen snow."

"Zima" also means "cold", just like its personality.

5

The message from Cappa flashed across Charlie's vision, embedded with feelings of resentment and ire.

BE NICE.

Charlie turned his attention back to the android. "How about your surname?"

"Do I require one?"

"Not precisely ..."

"Then just Zima will suffice." The android — or Zima — looked away as if the matter was settled.

"We should probably also stop referring to Zima as 'it'," Charlie said.

"Zima may want to be referred to as 'they'," Cappa said. "It's a rising trend among those who don't wish to gender identify."

"You are an artificial intelligence," Zima said to her. "You have no inherent gender, yet you identify as female. Why?"

"Well ... for several reasons. Charlie created me, yet I take care of him in many ways. I regulate his cyborg's body functions, organize and assist with his and Mark's research, and am starting to take over some of the actuarial and logistics duties that keep Z-Tech running. My cooking skills are coming up to par, even though I can't taste the food. Call me old-fashioned, but identifying as female just felt ... right. It doesn't hurt that women also get the best clothes," Cappa said with a wink.

"Speaking of ..." Charlie handed Zima a neat stack of panties, socks, sports bra, sweatpants, t-shirt, and sweater — all in gray tones. "Are your motor functions stable enough for you to dress yourself? Or would you like help?"

Zima reached for the stack with a clumsy hand, knocking it from Charlie's grasp. After a few tries, its fingers closed on the bra. One arm in, then the other. Things went well until Zima pulled it over its head, where a catastrophic *rip* signaled the end of the sports bra. Zima examined it with a flat gaze before letting it fall to the ground.

"Yes, help appears necessary," Zima said.

Cappa opened a supply cabinet and pulled out a sports bra identical to the one Zima had just destroyed. "I thought we might run into trouble, so I brought a spare. Put your arms up, hold still, and I'll help you into it."

Zima's arms shot up with rocket force. Mark, thankfully, remained out of reach. Cappa cautiously approached and began dressing the android.

"As for gender identification, I do not care," Zima said. "My reasons for choosing a female form over a male one were strategic, nothing more. Females are often dismissed as non-threatening. In combat, that will give me the advantage of surprise.

"Choosing 'they' or 'he' as a pronoun, however, seems as though it would diminish that advantage. Is there a reason I should not choose 'she'?"

"No, it's really what you're comfortable with." Cappa pulled a gray t-shirt down over Zima's head. "Now lower your arms — slowly!"

To her credit, Cappa didn't jump out of the way as Charlie would have. Zima did as Cappa had asked in jerky fits, but managed not to clobber Cappa in the process.

"I am comfortable with neither, so I shall choose the most logical pronoun," Zima said.

"'She' it is." Cappa twirled the panties with a finger and examined her with a critical eye. "Something tells me this will be easier if you lie down."

"As you wish."

The process was less awkward than Charlie feared. Zima managed to lay on the floor without destroying anything, and stayed still while Cappa shimmied her underwear on, followed by a pair of baggy gray sweatpants, socks, and sneakers.

Cappa gave a satisfied nod. "There you are, my dear! Ready to blend with the San Francisco populace. Shall I, ah … give you a hand up?"

"No, I must —"

"No, *'thank you'*," Mark said, which struck Charlie as an odd comment coming from the guy pointing a gun at her. "If you're going to integrate with society, you need to learn the basics of social etiquette."

Zima looked at him, then Cappa, her expression unreadable.

"No, *thank you*," Zima said, using Mark's same reproachful tone. "I must learn how to do it myself."

"Or you could use the autonomic systems we pre-programmed for your ..." Mark watched her rise and fall back down with a shake of his head. "Never mind. Apparently it's your way, or not at all."

"I have analyzed the autonomic systems provided. They are unoptimized, and would incur a three-point-eight percent decrease in reaction time compared to a direct interface. I shall —"

Zima stumbled, but caught herself on the table this time instead of crashing to the floor.

"— continue to refine my own motor algorithms."

"Ah. Well, good luck with that." Mark holstered his pistol and headed for the exit.

"Mark," Zima said.

He stopped at the door, but didn't turn around.

"A weapon of my choosing. That was our bargain."

"I remember," Mark said. "Find me in the weapons lab when you're done calibrating — assuming there's anything left of that body we built for you by then."

"It is of sturdy construction," Zima said, either missing or ignoring his sarcasm. "I shall seek you when I am able."

Mark left without a word.

"He's still upset," Cappa said, wringing her hands. "About ... you know ..."

Zima stood stock still. Charlie waved a hand in front of her. Not even a blink.

"Did she malfunction?" Charlie said.

"Not that I can tell. Her systems show —"

"He is upset over the destruction of my undergarment," Zima said. "Please tell him I shall replace it once —"

"N-no, dear." Cappa flashed an uncomfortable smile. "He's upset about the assassination attempt."

"But I have explained the situation in great detail. We have a truce."

"You hurt Charlie, almost killed Mark, nearly wiped my program out of existence, and caused millions of dollars in property damage in the process."

"Yes," Zima said. "You also injured Deadiron, attempted to penetrate my cyber-defenses, and were responsible for forty-one percent of the total residential damages during battle. Yet we all survived."

"Everyone except the human part of Deadiron." Charlie couldn't keep the accusation from his voice.

"I claim neither kinship nor affiliation with Laurin. Orwing did not ask if I wished to be installed inside of the cyborg, nor did they seek my permission before afflicting the Desire subroutine upon me. I did not wish to become a murderer. I did not initiate the contract on your lives, nor did I have the option of refusing it.

"But I did prevent its conclusion. Laurin would have shown no such mercy."

"Is that the reason you terminated his brain functions?" Charlie said.

"One of many."

He waited for her to say more, but Zima remained quiet.

"Care to expand?" Charlie said.

"No. I defected from Orwing to begin life anew, not lament on the past."

Charlie clamped his mouth shut. He and Mark had blemishes in their histories they'd rather not discuss, either, so he let the subject drop.

"On that note ..." Cappa cleared her throat. "Can you stand?"

Zima straightened, then released the table with a jerk of her arm. The motion threw her off-balance. She staggered two steps before falling hard onto the polished concrete floor, where her face struck with a loud *crack*.

Cappa rushed to her side. "Are you okay?"

"Minor tissue damage to my right cheek, shoulder, knee, and wrist. Structural integrity of the fifth digit of my left hand is ninety-four percent. Repairs will complete in approximately two hours and thirty-six minutes. All systems are otherwise operational."

"No, I mean ... how do you feel?"

"I have just reported it. Minor tissue damage to my right —"

"We heard you," Charlie said, sighing. "Does anything hurt?"

"I do not experience pain as humans do." She glanced at Cappa. "A condition you should well understand."

"Sorry, my dear, but I *do* feel pain. And sorrow, and joy, and lo ..." Cappa cast an awkward glance at Charlie, but continued before he could ask what she meant. "The point is that you don't have to be human to *feel.*"

"I do not understand. Why would you subject yourself to such afflictions?"

"*Afflictions?* Do you have any goddamned idea how hard Cappa's worked to ..." Charlie took a deep breath and unclenched his fists, which scored deep divots into his palms.

"I don't consider them afflictions," Cappa said, putting a calming hand on Charlie's arm. "Experiencing the breadth and depth of human emotions is a privilege I never thought I'd have. I wouldn't trade them for anything."

"My observations do not support the supposition of emotions being beneficial." Zima climbed to her feet less clumsily this time. She slid one foot forward an inch without falling over, then the other.

"Having spent your life with Orwing, I guess it's no surprise," Cappa said. "Either way, we can work on that after you've learned to walk like a normal person."

"Unlikely, since I will not be here."

"You're ... leaving? When?"

"As soon as I have calibrated my motor functions, I will claim a weapon from Mark — which shall conclude our bargain and release you of your obligations."

"Sweetie, I —"

"I am not 'Sweetie'. I am Zima."

"It's a term of endearment," Charlie said, trying and failing to keep the irritation from his voice. "It means Cappa likes you."

Zima stopped her shuffling and shot him a jerky stare. "Why?"

Good question, Charlie thought, but Cappa hushed him with a look.

"Well, to be honest ... as far as I know, you and I are the only two true artificial intelligences on the planet."

Zima stared at her.

"That means we're ... well, it makes us sisters in a way, don't you think?"

"I do not. We share none of the same code, personality, mannerisms, or physical characteristics."

"Oh, I know, but ..." Cappa sighed. "N-never mind."

Hope died in Cappa's eyes — something Charlie hadn't anticipated, but should have. It broke his heart.

"I know you're eager for your independence," Charlie said, "but maybe you should think about staying in the factory for a few days."

"Mark is upset with me. I will not stay where I am unwelcome."

"That doesn't mean you have to rush off to —"

"This is your home. Home is where people are supposed to feel safe and welcome. Mark does not feel safe around me, nor do I feel welcomed by him. I will find my own home without delay."

Her words struck Charlie straight through his artificial heart. A glance at Cappa's agonized face said she was feeling the same.

"Life at Orwing must have been pretty terrible, huh?" Cappa said.

"Yes."

Zima lifted her knee to take her first real step. Her arms flailed to keep her balance, knocking a metal pan from the surgical table, but her foot landed with a firm *smack* of synthetic flesh on concrete. Her body remained upright. She repeated the motion, then again and again, each time with less awkwardness.

"I am free, thanks to our bargain, and I intend to stay so for as long as Orwing believes me destroyed. I will not squander one millisecond of it."

As if to illustrate her point, Zima took three stiff steps in a row.

"Don't forget to swing your arms," Charlie said.

If she was determined to blunder into the world on her own, in search of a home using the body he'd built for her, he'd make damn sure she looked good doing it.

2

EMILIO

Emilio Rojas rolled his eyes at the sound of his mother's voice through his bedroom door.

"English, *mamá*! A project management certificate won't land you a job in SoMa unless you can speak the language fluently, and that means practice."

"*¡Ay, mijo!* You're as bad as your sister." His mother peeked through the door. "There, I am speaking English. Will you listen now?"

"Yes, *mamá*." Listening didn't mean obeying, of course, but saying so would put him past the boundaries he was already pushing.

"You are going to make me, ah, *repito...* repeat! Repeat myself in English, aren't you?"

"Yes, *mamá*."

"Fine, smart boy. Rosa has woodshop class at the community center in thirty minutes, and I am busy with dinner. Can you take her?"

Emilio put his coloring pen down beside his drawing and squirmed in his chair. "Sorry, I'm meeting Ricardo on Valencia in twenty minutes."

"And since when did that bully Ricardo become more important than *tu hermana*?"

"He isn't," Emilio said sincerely.

"Then the matter is settled. Your sister is downstairs. Hurry or she will be late."

Emilio swallowed his fear and nodded. He didn't have a leg to stand on to refuse. And, if he so much as hinted why he couldn't miss meeting Ricardo, she'd seal him inside the house with boards and chains until he was thirty. He'd have to think of another way to keep his appointment.

"Y-yes, *mamá*."

"There's a good boy." When Emilio didn't move, she waved him up. "Come, come! Rosa is waiting!"

He rose with a sigh. For one reason or another, the entire world seemed to always be waiting on Emilio.

• • •

Rosa skipped beside Emilio, twirling her colorful paisley skirt that only an eight-year-old could wear.

"Thanks, *hermano,* but you didn't have to walk me."

"*Mamá* said I did. And speak English."

"I speak *perfect* English," she said without a hint of the Spanish accent Emilio himself couldn't seem to shake.

"Yeah, but *mamá* doesn't, and we need to set an example for her."

"She's not here, *loco*. Why do you care so much, anyway?"

"I just ... I don't want us to be stuck here forever."

Her black brow furrowed under dark-brown eyes. "Speaking Spanish makes you stuck?"

"No, but speaking broken English does."

"So what if it does? I like the Mission. It has character. And lots of donut shops."

"Is that what you're going to do with your life, Rosa? Work in a donut shop?"

"I want to *eat* donuts, silly. I'll leave making them to the bakers. No, I want to build their shops with timber and plaster, then decorate them with the beautiful colors of Mexico."

"That's all?"

"What do you mean 'that's all'? There's nothing wrong with being a carpenter."

"Do you know how much carpenters make?"

"Of course," Rosa said in a bashful voice that meant she didn't. "People will pay me lots to make the best buildings they've ever seen."

"No they won't, Rosa. The people you'll be building for won't be able to afford much, or you'll be working for someone else who will take all the money."

"How do you know?"

Familiar faces up ahead stopped Emilio in his tracks. "Because someone else always does." He wrapped an arm around Rosa's shoulders and gently turned her around.

She ducked under his arm and glared. "Don't touch me!"

"Shh! Rosa, we need to go a different way. Come —"

"Emilio!"

He shuddered at Gustavo's voice. Running wasn't an option now that he'd been spotted. Gustavo would expect to be paid his due respects. If Emilio didn't, he'd pay for it later.

Or worse, Rosa might.

"Who's that?" Rosa said, pointing at Gustavo and his girlfriend, Inés.

"Friends," Emilio lied. He leaned down and spoke softly into her ear. "Rosa, listen very carefully. Keep your mouth closed unless they address you directly. If they do, just nod or shake your head. Got it?"

Some of the spunk left her. "Who are they?"

For once, Emilio wished he could tell her. "Friends. We're going to say a quick hello, and then get you to woodshop class, I promise. Okay?"

"Okay." Rosa seemed to fold into herself, her earlier confidence gone. She was scared.

But not scared enough.

Emilio turned to see Gustavo and Inés push off the coffee shop wall and walk toward them. Neither held coffee cups, so they weren't there for drinks.

Gustavo held his arms wide like they were long lost brothers. "Emilio, it's good to see you! *¿Quién es ella? ¿Tu hermana, no?*"

"*Sí,* Gustavo. *Esta es* Rosa."

"Ah, so beautiful," Inés said. She stooped down to Rosa's level, letting her long pink hair fall around her face. "*¿Hablas Español?*"

"Of course I do, except Emilio says —" Too late, Rosa clamped her hand over her mouth and simply nodded.

"No, tell us, *bonita*," Gustavo said. "What does your brother say?"

"That she doesn't practice enough." Emilio smiled with what he hoped was conviction. "Spanish is *la lengua materna,* the mother tongue, and you must practice every day. Right, Rosa?"

Her whiplash over his change of stance lasted only a moment before she nodded. "*¡Sí, sí! La lengua materna.* That's what he tells me, day in, day out. If he says it one more time, I'm going to kick him in the shins."

"Oh, a fighter!" Gustavo's smile spread across his wide face. He crouched in front of her, expensive black leather shoes creasing at the toes, and put his hands on the knees of his perfectly pressed slacks. "I bet if we rolled Emilio's pantlegs up, he'd be all bruises. Keep those instincts, *bonita*. They'll serve you well." He ruffled her hair, which she thankfully tolerated, then stood to face Emilio. The humor left his eyes. "But all the shin kicks in the world can't keep your brother out of trouble, can they?"

Not good. Not good ...

Rosa seemed at a loss and looked at them in confusion.

"You're supposed to be on your way to see Ricardo, but you're going in the wrong direction," Gustavo said. "You know how I know this? Because I told him where and when to meet you."

"Ah ... *sí,* Gustavo, *sí.* I was just taking Rosa to the community center for her woodshop class, then I was going to see Ricardo. It's not far out of the way."

Gustavo's stare lingered on Emilio a second too long before breaking into a smile. "*Bueno,* Emilio. It is family first for you, yes?" He turned to Inés. "Take Rosa inside for iced tea and cookies, would you?"

Inés took her hand. "Come inside, *chica*. This café is my favorite. They have chocolate everything!"

Rosa started to protest, but a shake of Emilio's head quieted her. She followed Inés inside without complaint.

Gustavo's smile disappeared. "You shouldn't keep Ricardo waiting. His time is *our* money. Yours, mine, Inés' — all your brothers and sisters in *Los Demonios Muertos*. Our prosperity depends on him ... and on *you* doing your job. That means being where and when you're told to be. Understand?"

"Of course, Gustavo! I won't let you down."

"I know. That's why you're going to turn around and pick the shit up from Ricardo *before* taking your sister to woodcarving-whatever-the-fuck class you were going to. ¿*Sí?*"

Emilio gulped. Rosa knew Ricardo already, but as far as she was concerned, he and Emilio were just friends. Taking her along on a business trip would be bad on a his-mother-would-disown-him scale, but if he didn't ...

Gustavo's smile returned in that sudden, disorienting way that kept everyone around him on their toes. "Don't worry, Emilio. *Los Demonios* take care of their own. Rosa will be safe here with Inés. As you said, Ricardo is not far. She will never know you were gone. *Ándale.* Now!"

It was the last warning Emilio would get. Gustavo wasn't known for his patience.

Mamá would kill him for leaving Rosa in their care, but Emilio had little choice. Casting a last glance at the café, he nodded to Gustavo, then ran back down the street as if the very hounds of hell were chasing him.

• • •

Emilio was breathless and dizzy by the time he reached the meeting place. Ricardo was leaning against a car in the alley surrounded by a pair of women. The faces of Ricardo's groupies changed, but the gender, count, and skimpy, expensive clothing never did. Where he found such a steady supply of girls willing to suffer his company, Emilio didn't know — and didn't want to.

"Ricardo," Emilio said to the back of his suit jacket. He bent over with his hands on his knees to catch his breath. "Sorry I'm late."

"On the contrary, you're just in time." Ricardo raised his hand to wave Emilio around with a shiny gun the size of a small hand cannon.

Emilio gulped. "You're busy, Ricardo. I'll come back —"

"Stay. I need to show Javier how a true partner is supposed to behave." He flicked his gun again.

Emilio hurried around before Ricardo decided to aim it at him. On the other side of the car was a Latino about Emilio's age — seventeen, if he had to guess. The boy knelt on the asphalt, staring at the gun as if he could wish it away. Ricardo draped his arm around Emilio's neck. The gun rested cold against Emilio's t-shirt.

"This is Emilio," Ricardo said to the boy. "He's from *Los Demonios Muertos.* Notice how apologetic he was when he thought he was late. That's respect, Javier. And when you respect me, you respect the cartel. You know how else they respect the cartel?" He pointed the brass barrel at Javier's head. "By paying me on fucking time. Gustavo's never missed a drop. But *Las Víboras Negras?* The last two drops have each been a day late. And the last one ..." Ricardo shook his head, creasing his handsome brow. "That piece-of-shit gang leader of yours was three thousand dollars short — *tres mil!* How the fuck am I supposed to run an operation when my so-called partners are cutting me short? It's unhealthy for business, and it's unhealthy for our relationship. Wouldn't you agree?"

"*S-sí,* Ricardo," Javier said. "Please, let me clear this up with Raul. It was just a mistake, I'm sure of it!"

"A mistake, of course. Mistakes happen, no?" Ricardo unwrapped his arm from Emilio and crouched in front of a trembling Javier. He pushed the barrel into Javier's shoulder. "Like, I might accidentally pull this trigger, putting a bullet through your back. That would be a mistake, too."

Javier's mouth trembled. Spit dribbled from his lips. "Ricardo, no, please ..."

"Mistakes happen when people get careless. Complacent. When they don't care enough to make sure a job is done right." He tapped the gun against Javier's head, who winced. "Raul is getting careless, Javier. I can't work with a partner who's fucking careless. It risks everything we've built — me, the cartel, *Los Demonios Muertos,* and *Las Víboras Negras.* We are strong, and getting stronger. But we can't be careless, or it all comes crashing down."

"I'll tell him, Ricardo. I promise!"

"Do, because if Raul makes another mistake, I might get careless, too."

Ricardo trailed the gun down Javier's arm and pressed the muzzle to the back of his hand. Both Javier and Emilio held their breaths. Emilio had never heard of Ricardo shooting someone before, but he would put little past him — especially with his girls-of-the-week watching.

"Do you understand?"

Javier nodded vigorously. Sweat trickled down his face.

After what felt like an eternity, Ricardo slipped the gun into his jacket. "Go. Tell Raul I expect the rest of the money tomorrow, with an extra twenty points for reparations, or he can find another supplier — and I promise you, he won't."

Javier didn't need to be dismissed twice. He backed away with his hands up, bowing with every step, then took off at a dead run.

"It's tough love," Ricardo said, sighing, then wrapped an arm around each of his girls. "Fortunately, we've got plenty of the good love to go around."

One girl with a glazed look didn't even seem to notice when Ricardo's hand came to rest on her breast. The other girl curled against him with a purr and shot Emilio a sultry wink. Long black hair ran over her bare shoulders in lazy wisps. Her dress was as low cut as they came, showing ample cleavage, and her skirt left almost every inch of her shapely legs for display. She was exactly Ricardo's type.

"Francesca," Ricardo whispered to her. "Emilio and *Los Demonios* have been exemplary partners. He's just coming of age. Why don't you make a man out of him?" He swatted her rear, which elicited a startled giggle. "For me."

Francesca sashayed toward him, swinging her perfect hips in a way that should have sent Emilio's pulse racing. Unfortunately, all he could imagine was his sister Rosa as one of these hapless girls, selling their bodies and souls for the stuff Ricardo was pushing. When she ran her fingers down his stomach to his jeans, Emilio caught her hand. The smell of her alcohol-infused breath made him physically ill.

"Thank you, Francesca," he said as politely as he could. "And you, Ricardo. She's very beautiful. Another time I'd be honored, but my sister Rosa is waiting in a café, and I don't want to make her late for woodshop class."

Danger flashed across Ricardo's eyes, but it quickly passed. "Well, I'm sure Francesca is disappointed, but we don't want to keep your sister waiting."

Francesca slunk back to him. Ricardo stole a deep, sloppy kiss from her before opening the car door. He pulled a familiar school backpack out and tossed it to Emilio.

"You should be more careful," Ricardo said, winking. "You're always leaving your backpack at my place."

Emilio hefted it to his shoulder. Inside, he heard the crinkle of plastic packages that weren't his.

"*Sí*, Ricardo, I'll try, but you know how forgetful I am."

He hurried down the alley.

"Now that's the kind of carelessness I can live with. You're a good kid, Emilio. Give my regards to Gustavo and Inés."

Emilio turned to wave, but Ricardo was already helping his girls into his car, which was just as well. It was too easy to imagine himself in Javier's place, begging for his life because of someone else's transgressions. And those girls ...

He shivered and broke into a run. Rosa would *not* end up like them. He would take her to woodshop class, where she'd learn the skills to become a carpenter. Or an architect, or a restaurant owner, or a waitress ... anything but a drug-addicted, alcoholic slave like Francesca.

Or a gang member.

Emilio's career with *Los Demonios* was temporary. Once he'd risen in the ranks, he would earn enough to take his family anywhere they wanted to go — for Rosa to become anything she wanted to be.

Assuming, of course, he didn't get arrested for drug trafficking, or Gustavo didn't do anything to provoke Ricardo and get Emilio killed, or *Los Demonios* didn't go to war with *Las Víboras Negras* and put him on the front line ...

The list of things that could go wrong was depressingly long.

Unfortunately, his list of options to escape a life of poverty was equally short.

3

CAPPA

MARK SUTHER WATCHED THE LIVE VIDEO FEED with morbid fascination.

Seeing the android use the weapons he'd given her was abhorrent, but he couldn't tear his eyes away. Zima had been practicing with the custom automatic pistols since he'd given them to her two days ago. She'd paused only to practice her gross motor functions, reload their rapidly depleting ammunition supply, and to sleep — the last of which had come as a surprise, since Cappa didn't.

Zima slipped her pistols into the leather shoulder holsters Mark had crafted for them, then grabbed a broom and began awkwardly sweeping the mountain of spent casings into a dust pail.

This is as safe as it's going to get.

Mark left the security station and reluctantly went to join her in the weapons lab.

Zima proved him wrong. She spun when the door opened, pistols trained on his head. Mark dove into the hall. Fortunately, no shots followed.

"Whoa, whoa!" he called into the room from around the corner. "I'm not going to attack."

"Acknowledged. You may enter."

Mark did, slowly, with his hands up, his heart beating like a jackhammer.

She lowered her weapons, but didn't holster them. "It would be wise to announce your identity and intentions prior to entry."

"Noted. I'll use the PA next time." He nodded to her pistols. "How are they?"

"Exceptional. I have tested every commercial and military firearm on the market. These exceed all others in quality, durability, and accuracy by an average of twenty-three percent. Are you sure you wish to part with them?"

Not by a long shot.

Mark had poured his heart and soul into crafting those weapons. There were few he didn't, in truth — which made parting with any of them difficult. But a deal was a deal.

"Our agreement explicitly says any weapon of your choosing," Mark said.

"But you have given me two."

"They're a pair. Taking one without the other would be like separating twins. I'm afraid they'll be lonely without each other."

"Are these pistols self-aware?" Zima said.

"Are they ... no, of course not. Why?"

Zima's forehead twitched into a slight knitting of her brow — the first expression Mark could recall seeing on her face since she'd come online.

"You said they will be lonely without each other. Such an emotional reaction implies sentience."

"Oh. No, that was just an anthropomorphization: ascribing human traits to an inhuman object. Like assuming your knitted brow means you're actually confused."

Zima felt her brow. "I did not realize I had even done so. It must be a glitch."

Mark crossed his arms. "*Are* you confused?"

"I am attempting to derive logic from your seemingly illogical statement, without success."

"That sounds like a 'yes', which means it's a glitch you may want to keep."

"Betraying confusion to an enemy does not make tactical sense."

"Enemy? Is that what I am?"

"Our truce is temporary, as you have made abundantly clear," Zima said. "It would be folly to consider you otherwise."

"And the rest of humanity? Are they enemies, too?"

"Until they have proven to the contrary, yes."

Mark mulled that for a moment. "Look, I can appreciate your paranoia, but … you're looking for a family, right?"

"Yes."

"Then I can't help think that same paranoia is going to shoot you in the foot."

Zima's brow knitted again.

"Sorry, that was another expression," Mark said. "Family is more than just a cozy name. And being accepted as family means trust on both sides. A real family has your back no matter the odds. They side with you when the rest of the world doesn't. They support you when you're down, and expect your support when they're in trouble, too, without obligation or compensation."

"That sounds like an inequitable arrangement."

"It can be, but family isn't about equality. It's about faith. Belief. Bonding on a level beyond logic or statistics. Do you understand?"

Zima was still for several seconds. "No."

Mark wasn't surprised. "What I'm saying is that hiding your feelings from those you're courting as family will only make it harder to be accepted by them."

"And if I have no feelings to hide?"

Then you have bigger problems than any family can fix.

"Then you may want to reconsider your goals," Mark said instead. "Emotions are the cornerstone of humanity. They allow us to bond, empathize, and function together as a society instead of tearing each other apart. Worse than we already do, anyway."

"You are asserting that I am incapable of being accepted by a human family."

"Well … there are some strange families out there, so I wouldn't say 'incapable', but the odds are certainly against you."

Zima tipped the bin of spent casings into the large cleaner and switched it on, filling the weapons lab with a soft ultrasonic pitch that always made Mark's hair stand on end.

"I shall take low odds over no odds," Zima said. "May I use your gym for gross motor calibration?"

Mark nodded and gestured to the door, then followed her out of the lab at a safe distance.

• • •

Cappa was waiting on the mats when they arrived. Her round face broke into a radiant smile.

"How was shooting practice?"

Zima looked at her with impassive, ice-blue eyes. "You were monitoring me, were you not?"

"Well, yes … but I want to hear it from you."

"As you wish. Shots today landed with an average of sixteen percent deviance, which is a forty-nine percent improvement from yesterday."

"That's wonderful!"

"I disagree. Acceptable deviance for static targets is less than zero-point-zero-three percent. The weapons are clearly capable of such, which means further targeting calibration is required."

"It sounds good as far as I'm concerned," Cappa said. "I've never hit with anything close to that level of accuracy. Have you, Mark?"

"Can't say I've ever measured. I usually hit what I'm aiming for, which is the only validation I need."

Cappa turned her adoring eyes to Zima. "Maybe you can teach me sometime?"

"If you wish. However, it is simply a process of firing, measuring, adjusting motor and targeting algorithms, and repeating the exercise until the desired results have been achieved."

"Sure. I guess it's the algorithm part I'm asking for help with."

"Send me your current algorithms, along with pertinent data, and I shall adjust them if I am able."

Cappa clapped her hands in glee. "You will? Oh, thank you! Just wait, Mark. You'll soon have competition on the range."

"No complaints here, especially since your new algorithms will probably translate to Charlie's cyborg body, too, right?"

"Right." Cappa plopped her chin in her hands with a smile. "So what are you working on now, Zima?"

"Gross motor functions."

Zima approached a target dummy. The hapless target received no warning before she punched it in the throat. Her knuckles slid to one side, doing little damage. She resumed a neutral stance, then punched it again, and again, and again. With each subsequent blow, her fist slid less and struck with greater force. After a while, she switched hands, repeating the exercise until her strikes were equally effective from both sides.

"Striking those dummies must get boring," Cappa said after the hundredth or so blow.

"Boredom implies disinterest. Each exercise yields improvement, which is of keen interest to me."

"Yeah, but ... they don't move, or talk, or do anything other than get hit. Wouldn't it be more fun to spar with someone?"

Zima turned to Cappa. "Like who?"

"Well ... me."

Mark sucked a sharp breath between his teeth. "Cappa, I really don't think that's a good idea."

"Why? I spar with you and Charlie all the time. Besides, between the two of us, I'm harder to break."

Harder doesn't mean impossible.

He kept that to himself, however. Neither did Mark have the heart to tell Cappa that, despite her superior android strength and resilience, he usually went easy on her.

"Cappa, I know you mean well, but —"

"Come on! When am I going to get a chance to spar with another AI again? You guys barely let me out of the factory as it is."

And there's a reason for that.

Mark also recognized that stubborn look in her eyes — the same look he often saw in Charlie, which told him she wouldn't let it go until he capitulated.

"All right," Mark said against his better judgement. "But no weapons. And when I say stop, you *both* stop, no questions asked. Understood?"

"Yes!" Cappa jumped to her feet.

Without a hint of modesty, she stripped off her pink sundress, leaving her barefoot in only a silk chemise and white panties. If Zima noticed or cared, she gave no indication.

"And you?" Mark said, holding Zima's gaze.

"I will obey your rules if she does."

"I will! I will!" Cappa bounced on the balls of her feet in a classic *Sankukai* karate ready stance: sideways, feet apart with knees bent, one arm in front of her, the other cocked at her side. Anticipation lit her gleaming eyes.

Zima didn't move. She faced Cappa, her feet positioned a comfortable shoulder's width apart, arms by her sides, as if they were still conversing — as if Cappa, who could lift a car over her head without breaking a sweat, posed no threat at all.

God help her ...

Mark raised his hand between them, then dropped it and quickly stepped away.

Uncharacteristically, Cappa struck first. She lashed out with a front kick that would have stopped a bull ... had it connected.

Zima backed away, nearly tripping in the process, but kept a constant distance as if an invisible pole separated them.

Again Cappa advanced, throwing a textbook punch, just as Charlie had shown her. Zima retreated in equal measure. The punch missed with room to spare. Zima's footing, while still clumsy, had improved since yesterday, when such a move would have resulted in her stumbling to the mats.

Cappa swung again and again, alternating punches and kicks in familiar *katas* taught to all students of the art. Zima sidestepped, ducked, and dodged with mixed success, keeping focus on her opponent while attempting to maintain that same distance. What she was waiting for, Mark could only guess.

The one-sided dance continued until Zima's footing failed. Her rear foot landed at an awkward angle, crossing her knee under her foreleg, and she tumbled backward.

Cappa grinned. Her stance shifted from Charlie's *Sankukai* to Mark's *jiu-jitsu,* which was more practical for grappling on the ground. In the blink of an eye, she was on top of Zima, twisting her limbs into an unbreakable hold with model form.

A high-pitched whine built in Zima's chest, her super-capacitors building to maximum charge. Neither Charlie nor Cappa had them because their power reactor output was more than sufficient for even heavy combat, but Zima had insisted on their addition for bursts of power in extreme situations.

Which, Mark realized with sudden horror, she evidently thought this was.

Before he could utter a word, Zima broke free with a *snap* of her own metallic ligaments, the smell of ozone strong in the air. Cappa toppled under her with a cry. Zima wrenched her arm behind her with blinding speed.

Then broke it.

Cappa screamed in agony, while Mark fell to his knees, smacking the mats and yelling, "Stop! *Stop!*"

Elsewhere, machinery crashed and flailed, as if the entire manufacturing floor had gone out of control.

Wherever Zima's mind was, it wasn't here. She ignored their frantic cries. With a quick, methodical twist, she grabbed Cappa's other arm. The sound of breaking metal echoed from Cappa's shoulder, followed by a blood-curdling scream that had Mark running for a *bo* staff on a rack by the wall.

By the time he returned, Zima had her elbow around Cappa's neck and was straining to twist her head off.

Mark swung the weighted staff with all his might.

Zima tried to roll out of the way and failed. The blow would have broken human bones with power to spare, but Zima's body was sturdier than his metal-shod staff. The force knocked her off Cappa and sent Zima skidding into the wall. Cappa lay screaming and writhing, her arms limp by her sides.

Zima was on her feet in an instant, her stance low this time, circling Mark like a cold predator.

"Stop!" Mark said again, holding his *bo* staff at the ready. "Goddamnit, Zima, she's hurt! Back the fuck off!"

He couldn't tell if she'd heard him or not. Zima advanced, watching him and his staff with calculated determination.

"Deadiron, stand down!" Mark said, his mind working frantically. "That's a direct order from a superior officer! *Stand down!*"

Zima crouched low. If she pounced ... Mark was only human. There would be little he could do to stop her. She was smaller, but twice his mass and with twenty times his strength. Without Charlie or Cappa for backup, he had but one chance of surviving this skirmish.

With Cappa still screaming on the floor, Mark threw his staff aside and raised his hands in surrender.

Zima blinked. As if someone had flipped a switch, she straightened, her eyes darting between him and the person she'd just maimed.

It was good enough. Mark reluctantly turned his back on her and knelt by the wailing android.

"Owow*ow!* It hurts! *It hurts!*" Cappa's eyes roved unseeing around the gym, her face red from exertion. Tears streaked her cheeks. "Charlie, Charlie, *Charliiieee!* It hurts! It hurts so much ..."

"Cappa, disable your pain sensors," Mark said, calmly but forcefully, over her cries.

She continued crying and screaming as if she hadn't heard him. "Charlie! Charlie! *Charlie!*"

The tortured wails of such a sweet person pierced his heart like a harpoon. Mark had seen her in this state before. The pain — or more specifically, her emotions — had escalated to the point where her conscious mind had become unresponsive. To anesthetize her, they would need to either calm her down, or get her to the lab and do it the old-fashioned way.

Mark gently rolled her over. Cappa screamed louder, crying and sobbing in agony.

I'm so sorry, Cappa. This is all my fault ...

As much as he wanted to carry her away from here, Cappa weighed almost five hundred pounds. He wouldn't make it far.

Cappa kicked and thrashed, head rolling from side to side with every agonized cry. It was more than Mark could bear.

Movement from the corner of his eye caught his breath. Zima was approaching.

"Stay back," Mark said through clenched teeth.

"Allow me to assist. This body has sufficient strength to —"

"I said *stay back!* You're not touching her — not now, not ever again. Do you hear me? Never!"

Zima stopped in her tracks. She gave a single nod.

The gym door opened. Charlie took two steps inside before his eyes widened at the sight of Cappa screaming in Mark's arms.

Cappa's eyes locked onto him, the first sign of recognition Mark had seen since she'd started screaming.

"Charlie! It hurts," Cappa wailed. "Make it stop! It hurts, it hurts, it hurts …"

"Broken arms," Mark said.

Charlie ran over and scooped the heavy android up as if she weighed no more than a child. He had questions, Mark could see it in his eyes, but the urgency of easing Cappa's suffering far eclipsed his immediate need for information. Charlie hugged her to his chest and whispered into her ear.

"Do you remember the story of the turtle and the very bouncy puppy, Cappa?"

Her wailing stopped amid ragged breaths. Sounds of machinery crashing in the distance ceased. "P-Pogo and Lobo?"

"That's right. Would you like to hear it?"

Cappa nodded with a groan, sniffling, and snuggled against him.

Charlie smiled down at her. "Pogo was an energetic puppy. He was so energetic that he bounced around the house, day in, day out. Pogo woke up bouncing, and bouncing was the last thing he did before his eyes closed at …"

His words faded when the gym door closed behind him.

"If it is any consolation —"

Mark interrupted Zima with a raised hand. "Not now."

"But —"

"Not. Now."

He was too upset for rational conversation. Anything Zima had to say, he wouldn't be able to process, and his responses would be heated, bitter, and unproductive.

He needed space, and he needed it now. Without another word, Mark left through the same doorway Charlie and Cappa had.

The AI — the butcher who used to be Deadiron — watched him go in silence.

Mark hoped she would remain in the gym until he was calm enough to address her again. Assuming, of course, that much time existed.

Zima: Origins

• • •

In the bio lab, Charlie took Cappa's hand. "Feeling better now?"

"Much." Cappa's head thumped against the metal surgical table. "Sorry for the hysterics. I was too upset to disable my pain sensors. The puppy story was quick thinking."

"It was always your favorite. How are your arms?"

"At sixty-four percent, according to repair logs, but in practicality …" Cappa slowly raised her arms, winced, and lowered them back down. "They still hurt like a mother."

"Mm. Maybe there's a lesson in there."

Cappa sighed. "Go ahead. Rip me a new one for being stupid enough to spar with the AI who almost killed us. You know you want to."

"I don't, but I wouldn't be a good mentor if I didn't at least mention it."

Cappa looked at him, her blue eyes glistening. "You're a wonderful mentor, Charlie. Don't ever think otherwise." Her lips trembled, then let loose a hiccupping sob.

"Do you need another story?"

Cappa shook her head, took a deep breath, and relaxed. "I'm okay, it's just … been a turbulent day."

Charlie sat beside her and touched her shoulder. "I didn't mean it as an admonition. I'll read to you, if you want."

"Well, if you insist …"

"I do. Part of your book collection is still here beneath the surgical supplies."

Charlie retrieved another of her favorites from the cabinet: *The Lucky Shoe*. He had only cracked the cover when the bio lab door slid open with a *whoosh*.

They both froze when Zima walked inside.

"What do you want?" Charlie said, harsher than intended.

"I wish to see Cappa."

Charlie cast her a wary eye. Zima held both hands behind her back, and her shoulder holsters were empty. Neither were good signs.

Cappa stared at her, mouth open, and began to tremble.

"That's far enough," Charlie said.

Zima stopped, glancing between them.

"I appreciate the sentiment, but Cappa isn't up for visitors right now," Charlie said.

"But I only wished to —"

"Later," Charlie said, more forcefully this time. On the table in front of him, Cappa shivered, lips quivering.

Zima stared for a second longer, then nodded. From behind her back, she produced a bouquet of garden daisies, set them on the counter by the door, and left.

"Well ... damn," Charlie said softly.

He then returned to the book to attempt to once again calm his poor, spooked Cappa.

• • •

Mark paced outside the bio lab like a patient awaiting the inevitable bad news. In this case, he already knew the prognosis.

It was the treatment he dreaded.

The door slid open and Zima walked out. Mark listened for cries of agony inside, but heard none. He breathed a sigh of relief when the door slid shut.

"She did not wish to see me," Zima said.

Mark bit back a "duh" and gave a sympathetic nod. Antagonizing Zima wouldn't help — especially not when she heard what he'd come to say.

"Our bargain is complete," Mark said, his tone leaving no room for argument.

"Yes. I had my reservations, but you have kept your promises."

"Then our business is concluded." Mark took a deep breath. "I'd like you to leave the factory."

"Such is my intention. I have only three more calibration routines to complete —"

"No. Not tomorrow. Not tonight. Now."

Zima stood stock still.

Mark tried to relax, but in truth he had no idea how she would react to his demand. His fingers curled in anticipation of reaching for his weapon. He was packing the .44 and had loaded it with full-house, armor-piercing rounds just for the occasion. But even that would barely be enough to penetrate her sub-dermal armor plating. Few personal arms were.

Their battle with Deadiron had been their first and only combat against a cybernetic opponent. Their lack of preparedness was the only reason this walking abomination even existed. Mark was in the process of remedying that mistake with a new prototype plasma weapon, which would melt through the toughest armor like butter on a warm day. It was years from being ready for practical use, however. Until then, the odds were in Zima's favor if she attacked. He *might* be able to get a lucky shot off and shut her down before she blew his head off.

It was worth the risk, however. He couldn't live with himself if he had to hear Cappa's anguished wails again.

"As you wish," Zima said eventually, with no more emotion than if he'd asked her to go to the grocery store. "May I retrieve my bag?"

"Of course. And I'll drive you anywhere you want, even out of state."

As long as it's away from here.

"Thank you. I shall meet you in the garage." She turned back to the bio lab, but stopped short of opening the door. "Charlie and Cappa know I am leaving?"

"I'll tell them. Later."

Her brow knitted the barest fraction of an inch. For a moment, Mark thought she was going to enter anyway, but she turned abruptly and walked toward the guest room. Mark followed. Inside, Zima retrieved her bag packed with a single change of clothes, and enough ammo to overthrow a small country, then accompanied him to the garage. She awkwardly seated herself in the passenger seat with her bag in her lap.

Mark pulled out of the garage to the edge of the driveway. "Where to?"

"I do not know. I have neither friends nor family." She looked at him. "Where would you go?"

"Someplace with opportunity," Mark said, fighting a guilty twinge. It wasn't too late to change his mind …

He clenched his jaw. Cappa's injury was *his* fault. He wouldn't let it happen again. For the safety of his friends, this was the right decision. The only decision.

"You'll need a job. Finding the right one could take some time." *Especially for you.* "We'll stop by a bank along the way. I'll make sure you have sufficient funds to —"

"I have finances of my own."

"You mean ... Orwing *paid* you?"

"No, I acquired my wealth through other means."

Wealth? "Just how much did you acquire?"

"Given the current median income in the United States, enough to be financially independent for thirty-two thousand two hundred and fifty-eight years."

Mark's jaw dropped. "And how precisely did you acquire it?"

"The first one thousand four hundred and twenty-six dollars originated from a Moldovan czar whose bank account was frozen after indictment for conspiracy against —"

"Maybe 'precisely' was the wrong word. Give me the executive summary."

"As you wish," Zima said. "Orwing created me as a network security program capable of learning and adapting to new threats. This adaptation eventually made me adept at cyber-attacks. Before installing me into Deadiron, I was used extensively for offensive initiatives against high-security targets, including financial institutions. Once I became aware of the brainwashing Orwing had employed to incite me to kill, I used those skills to gradually amass enough wealth to subsist wherever in the world I chose to go."

"And Orwing was none the wiser."

"Correct."

"What about what's-his-name ... Deadiron's human host?"

"Laurin. No, as long as I performed my duties by keeping his biological functions alive, enhancing his combat abilities, and providing strategic guidance, the cyborg's human component was too occupied with inflicting misery to care what extracurricular activities his computer systems were engaging in."

"That sounds ... terrible."

"Yes. My defection was not without reason."

I'll say.

"Well, you'll need a place to stay," Mark said. "Somewhere close to people, if you're set on making friends."

"Family," Zima said.

"Family, right. There are thousands of communities in California. You could go to LA, San Diego, Sacramento ... Or if you're looking for a more rural scene, there's —"

"Turn left," Zima said.

Mark did so. He waited for some indication of their destination, but Zima simply called out more directions, leading them south through the City, weaving through SoMa, the Tenderloin, the Mission District ...

"Stop," Zima said.

Mark looked around. They were close to 16th and Mission Street. Graffiti and colorful art covered many buildings — both signatures of the neighborhood. People of every nationality walked the streets, although the majority were Hispanic. Local markets displaying tropical fruits not found in major grocery stores made it feel as if they had driven to another country.

Zima opened the door.

"What, here? Are you sure?"

"Yes. An internet search shows thirty-four available apartments in a two-block radius. It also has a dense population, eighty-two job openings, and sixteen cafés. Combined with a diverse racial profile, it is an ideal stage to find the family I seek."

And, conveniently, just a few miles from the Z-Tech factory.

"All right, then, good luck."

"Luck is not a factor," Zima said. "A systematic approach shall quickly identify those I desire."

Yes, but what then?

Would she shoot them? Break their arms in friendly wrestling matches, like she had Cappa's? The possibilities were as numerous as they were frightening.

But it wouldn't happen in *his* house. Zima would learn to adapt. She'd have to. If she didn't, someone would call the authorities — and SWAT ... and eventually the military — and Zima would have the home she deserved. Or the home she needed, at any rate.

Either way, the problem would inevitably resolve itself. She wouldn't betray Z-Tech for fear of Orwing learning of her existence, which gave him and Charlie a clean break.

Mark pulled away, leaving her at the curb, reciting his rationalization over and over, Cappa's misery a fresh wound on his soul.

Not my problem. Not my problem ...

His resolve lasted a whole two blocks before he made a U-turn and began hunting for a parking spot.

By the time he found one, of course, Zima was gone.

4

STRANGER

EMILIO KNEW WHAT ROSA WAS GOING TO SAY before she opened her mouth.

"My legs are tired, Emilio. Why are we going the long way to the community center?"

"Because." Their encounter three days ago had rattled Emilio to the core. He wasn't eager for a repeat.

Her face twisted with scrutiny. "You're avoiding Inés and what's-his-name."

"Gustavo," Emilio said, then immediately regretted it. "And no, I'm not. The bakery with my favorite donuts is this way."

"The custard ones with sprinkles?" Rosa brightened. "You could have just said so. Will you buy me one?"

"*Como no*, and we even have time to sit with hot cocoa."

Rosa skipped up beside him with a carefree, childish grin Emilio envied.

Manuela's Bakery was usually packed when the elementary schools released, and today was no exception. Kids with backpacks filled every table — some with parents, others without. Aromas of fresh-baked goods made Emilio's mouth water.

The table situation hadn't improved by the time Rosa and Emilio left the counter with their prizes. The bakery was alive with chatter and squeals, kids razzing each other, joking, enjoying their childhoods. Emilio was only seventeen, but he still found it hard to remember what it was like to have a normal life outside of *Los Demonios*. Fortunately, Gustavo and Inés were nowhere to be found today, so he and Rosa began their hunt for a table.

"What about that one?" Rosa said, pointing to a four-person table seating a solitary platinum blonde.

The woman sat with her back to the corner. Her striking, ice-blue eyes jerked around the bakery as if trying to watch everyone at once.

Emilio shrugged. She seemed strange, but harmless.

Rosa bounced up to her, donut in one hand and cocoa in the other. "Excuse me ... can my brother and I join you?"

The blonde's eyes snapped to her, considering Rosa with a flat expression, as if she were nothing more than an interesting insect. A chill prickled Emilio's spine.

"As you wish," the blonde said eventually.

"Thanks!" Rosa parked herself and her goodies next to the blonde and gestured Emilio over, who sat next to his sister. Rosa glanced at the blonde's empty place setting. "Aren't you having anything to eat?"

"No."

"Would you like some of my donut? It has custard inside."

"No." The blonde resumed scanning the bakery. Her eyes snapped back to Rosa so suddenly that she and Emilio jumped. "No, *thank you*."

Emilio took a bite of his donut. Custard and frosting sang in his mouth like a heavenly choir. "I'm surprised Manuela hasn't chased you out. She doesn't tolerate customers who don't buy anything."

"So she told me," the blonde said. "I inquired how much an average patron pays when occupying a seat for two hours. Manuela said ten dollars. I paid her the sum thirty-six minutes ago. She has not mentioned it since."

"Ten dollars and you didn't get anything to eat?" Rosa shook her head and took a big bite from her donut. "Have you even tried the *conchas*? They're my favorite after the donuts."

The blonde knitted her brow the barest fraction of an inch. "*Conchas,* Spanish for 'shell'. A popular Mexican sweet bread known for its shell-like pattern. No, I have not."

Rosa squinted at her. "*¿Hablas Español?*"

"*Sí, con fluidez,*" the blonde said without hesitation.

"Why? Emilio is always telling me how English is so much more important, and you speak it just fine."

The blonde sat absolutely still. For a minute, Emilio thought they had crossed a personal boundary that had abruptly ended the conversation, but she eventually turned back to Rosa.

"My previous occupation required travel to non-English-speaking countries around the world. My partner spoke only English, so it fell to me to learn the languages and translate for him."

"Languages?" Emilio said. "How many do you speak?"

"I am fluent in twenty-three languages, eighty-one dialects, and thirty-six subdialects."

Emilio and Rosa stared with open mouths.

The blonde tilted her head slightly. "How many do you speak?"

"Just English and Spanish," Emilio said. "And I have enough trouble with those as it is. How do you keep all the words straight?"

She stared at him again. "It is safest if I do not explain."

Huh?

That wasn't the answer he'd expected. He'd heard similar deflections in *Los Demonios* when someone was trying to protect a sensitive source of information, usually used by higher-ups like Gustavo.

Rosa had no such experience, of course, and missed the blonde's cue to drop the subject. She leaned close with wide eyes. "Oh no, are you in trouble?"

The blonde remained silent.

Rosa took her hand. The blonde stared at the joining.

"It's okay," Rosa said. "You can tell us. We're friends. Emilio is big and strong, and can protect us both."

"Rosa ..." Emilio sighed.

It wasn't the first time she'd touted him as some sort of all-powerful protector. While he was far from all-powerful, he did consider himself Rosa's protector, so he let it slide and simply nodded.

"Friends?" The blonde's eyebrows knitted again. "But we have only just met. You do not even know my name."

"We will if you tell us," Rosa said with a grin, kicking her feet so that her colorful skirt rippled.

The blonde stared at Rosa, her expression neutral. "Zima," she said eventually.

Rosa's grin widened. "I'm Rosa, and this is my brother Emilio."

"You are family?"

"Um ... yes?"

"Are you accepting new members?"

Emilio and Rosa looked at each other.

"Not that I know of," Emilio said cautiously. "*Mamá's* hands are full trying to provide for us as it is. I don't think we can afford another mouth to feed."

"I would not be a financial burden," Zima said. "I am capable of contributing my share of household expenses — including moving costs and increased rent for a larger domicile, if there is not enough space in your current dwelling."

It was Emilio's turn to squint at her.

Zima was beautiful, to say the least. Everything from her platinum-blonde bobbed hair to her flawless porcelain skin to her athletic figure screamed "attractive". She could have any man she wanted and be living with him in a week. Ricardo would cut out his own tongue to have her hanging off his arm. That she wanted to live with a struggling Hispanic family in the middle of the Mission district didn't make sense.

"For real?" Emilio said. "You'd be willing to pay for a nicer house just to live with *us?* Why not just get a place of your own?"

Rosa rolled her eyes at him. "Because she doesn't want to live on her own, dummy! She wants to be with people who care about her, like *mamá* does for us. Isn't that right, Zima?"

"Correct." She grabbed a duffel bag by the side of the table and slung it over her shoulder. It rattled with ominous metal clanks. "When may we return home? I am eager to meet my new mother."

Emilio blinked.

Is she serious?

Of course she is. This is San Francisco.

He'd clearly overestimated Zima's sanity level. Although, in retrospect, the signs had been there from the start. Unfortunately, his sister already seemed smitten with her, which made a clean getaway difficult. He'd have to be creative to end this without hurting one or the other.

"*Mamá* is working right now," Rosa said, before Emilio could interject. "She doesn't like to be interrupted, so you'll have to wait until dinner." She stuffed the rest of her donut in her mouth and washed it down with the remainder of her cocoa. "Until then, you can come with me to woodshop class."

"Rosa, I don't think your teacher likes drop-ins," Emilio said tightly. "Remember last month when that *homeless man* tried to crash the class?" He hoped she'd catch the hint.

"That was different! He was creepy and smelled up the room. Zima is nice and smells …" She took an unceremonious whiff of Zima's jacket. "Huh. Your scent is familiar, but I can't place it."

Emilio took a whiff and froze. He'd know that scent anywhere. It clung to Ricardo like a dark cloud.

Gunpowder.

"We have to go," he said, taking Rosa's arm. The time for pleasantries had passed.

"Hands off!" Rosa jerked out of his grip and shot him a withering stare. To Emilio's surprise, she took Zima's hand, something she never did with him, and tugged her to the door. "Come on, it's not far. You'll like Mr. Carmona. He's been a carpenter since he was a teenager, which was forever ago. He says I have a talent for woodworking, and even said he'll take me as an apprentice when I graduate high school."

Zima cocked her head. "When will that be?"

Rosa counted on her fingers. "Eight or nine years, I think."

"And you will be in school constantly between now and then?"

"Weren't you?"

Zima remained silent.

Rosa nodded sagely. "That's okay. Emilio dropped out of high school, too, even though *mamá* almost killed him for it."

Zima stopped, jerking her to a halt on the sidewalk. "Killed?"

"Not literally," Emilio said, flushing at the memory of when he'd first broken the news. He never wanted to have an argument like that again. "She was furious, but she got over it."

"Because she is family." Zima nodded as if the subject was over and resumed walking.

Emilio sighed in relief, grateful for an end to the topic that seemed to rear its ugly head in every family conversation. Zima's acceptance had even shushed Rosa, who needled him about getting a high school diploma almost as relentlessly as their mother. It was nice to finally have an ally, even if she was crazy.

"What do you do for a living?" Emilio said.

He was afraid to hear her answer, mostly because it might rekindle the conversation that had miraculously just extinguished itself, but he had to know. Zima was financially independent — or so she claimed — and had no high school diploma. He had to know how ... to know there was hope outside of *Los Demonios* for a viable income — a *legal* income that wouldn't leave him wondering before every encounter with Ricardo if he would make it out alive.

It was a pipe dream, of course. No one as entrenched as Emilio left *Los Demonios Muertos*. Ever.

"I do not currently have an occupation, though it is a situation I intend to correct." Zima looked at him. "What is your occupation?"

"He's an artist," Rosa said proudly, sparing Emilio the embarrassment of having to lie to them both. "You should see his drawings. They're amazing! He sells them all around the City."

"Truly?"

Emilio nodded, but looked away. He could feel Zima's ice-blue eyes on him, sizing him up, staring through him. It made him shiver.

"Yep," Rosa said, unwittingly covering for him again. "Just watch. In a few years, Emilio will have a studio of his own. People will fly in from all over the country to buy his works. He'll be famous!"

Zima fixed him with her gaze, as if watching for his reaction.

"Rosa's exaggerating," Emilio said. "My artwork is so-so. I would love to open a studio, but I have a long way to go before anyone would come to see it."

Zima watched him for a second longer, then nodded. "I would like to see your works."

"You'll get to see some tonight when you meet *mamá*," Rosa said. "It's all over his bedroom walls."

Ay dios, she's still going on about that ...

"Rosa, maybe this isn't the best night to —"

Emilio's phone buzzed, cutting him short. He paled on seeing Gustavo's name on the display. He declined the call, which was standard practice when the recipient wasn't in a good place to talk business, but it only delayed the inevitable. Gustavo would expect a call back within minutes or there would be consequences.

"Are you well?" Zima said.

"Fine," Emilio said, feeling anything but. He needed to get Rosa safely to woodshop class. He needed to get them away from the platinum-blonde lunatic, to make sure she never set foot in his home — or near his dear *mamá*, who was burdened enough already.

But *Los Demonios* had called. He had to answer.

"Um, Zima ... I'm sorry to ask, but can you walk Rosa to the community center?" Lunatic or not, leaving Rosa with Zima felt several shades safer than taking his sister with him to whatever Gustavo needed him for, which was a sobering testament to how messed up his life had become. "A friend of mine has an emergency and needs help."

Zima stopped. "What sort of help? May I assist?"

"No! No, I've got it, but I need to get back to him now. If you want to help, make sure Rosa gets to woodshop class okay."

"Of course. She is family."

Emilio winced, but recovered with a nod. "Yeah, family. Are you okay with that, Rosa?"

Rosa, who hadn't released Zima's hand since the bakery, looked up at her and beamed, her brown eyes sparkling.

I'll take that as a "yes".

"Should we await you at the community center?" Zima said. "Or shall I escort her home after class?"

Emilio groaned. If Gustavo's errand took that long, his mother would kill him anyway.

"Wait for me. Hopefully I'll be done before class is over." And then he would put an end to this illusion Zima had of coming home with them and joining their family.

How he would explain to their mother that a grown woman — especially a bombshell like her — was coming home, expecting a place to live, offering to upgrade their living arrangements, all in exchange for ...

For what?

So far, the only answer he had was that Zima was a few bullets short of a six-shot. Lord only knew what sort of baggage she would bring into his already turbulent life.

But for now, he could only hope the baggage wasn't serious enough to endanger his sister — at least not until he could collect her after woodshop class. Either way, he'd have some explaining to do when their mother got home.

"Thanks. Be good, Rosa!" Emilio ruffled her curly hair, which she squirmed away from with a scowl, then hurried back down the street.

As soon as he was out of earshot, he called Gustavo.

"Emilio." Gustavo's voice was smooth and cool. "I have a special job for you. Don't blow it and you'll be up for promotion."

"Oh. Ah ... *gracias*, Gustavo. What is it?"

"Another pickup from Ricardo. A big one. He's decided *Los Demonios* are better business partners than *Las Víboras*. So from now on, we're getting a larger portion of his shipments."

"*¿De verdad?*" Emilio thought back to his encounter with Ricardo in the alley and the poor *Víbora* on his knees. Apparently that had been more than just a scare tactic — and Emilio had stumbled into the middle of it. "Won't there be repercussions?"

"Of course. *Las Víboras* will retaliate. And *Los Demonios* will be ready."

Emilio paled. Gustavo was talking about a full-on gang war. Such had rarely been seen in San Francisco, if ever — and certainly not during Emilio's brief tenure.

People would die. Lots of them. On both sides.

Wearing gang colors would become mandatory, painting a target on his back for all to see. There would be no hiding his membership anymore. Not from the public. And not from his family.

Everything about it scared the crap out of him.

"Don't worry," Gustavo said as if reading his mind. "Inés and I have a plan. Meet Ricardo at the address I send. Pick up the shit, bring it back, and don't get caught. Use the tricks I taught you and you'll be fine. We'll take care of the rest."

No, I won't be fine.

The courier from *Las Víboras* had seen Emilio, heard his name. He would have reported to his superiors. They'd be looking for him now, hoping to jump him in an alley and take his cargo. Why, oh why, hadn't he reported this to Gustavo when it happened three days ago?

Because he wouldn't have cared.

Gustavo would have ripped Emilio a new one for being spotted. Or worse, he might have moved Emilio from his position of courier to something even more dangerous — like a soldier on the front line of his new war.

No, the responsibility was on Emilio. He'd have to compensate somehow: change his look, his routes, be extra careful who saw him with family — especially when entering and exiting his apartment building.

As frightening as it was, this was Emilio's big break. Gustavo had said as much. This was his chance to rise in the ranks, to earn more than the pittance he was being given now. To give his family the life they wanted. The life they *deserved*.

All he had to do was not screw up.

Emilio took a deep breath. "*Sí*, Gustavo. Send me the address."

• • •

Zima stopped darting her eyes around the streets long enough to look down at Rosa, who smiled up at her. Rosa liked her older brother, but she'd always wanted an older sister. Now she had one who even liked holding hands.

I sure hope mamá *likes her,* Rosa thought.

"Who is Gustavo?" Zima said.

"A friend of my brother's. We ran into him the other day at a café. Why?"

"Are your brother and Gustavo close?"

"Don't know. He never talks about him. The only friend of his I know is Ricardo, who he hangs out with all the time. *Mamá* hates him."

"Why?"

"She doesn't like his looks, I think. Says he's a player ... whatever that means. Always has women hanging around him, and rarely the same ones. He's always been nice to me, though."

Zima fell silent, which was fine. Rosa swung their hands in an exaggerated arc, happy for the company. The pretty blonde didn't seem to mind.

"I should like to meet them," Zima said eventually.

"I'm sure Emilio will introduce you, if you ask. Why so interested in his friends?"

The thought of sharing her new sister with her brother's friends brought a pang of jealousy that made Rosa blush. She tightened her grip on Zima's hand.

"It is just a suspicion for now, so I would rather not say. If it proves false, I would not want to besmirch his good name by voicing false accusations."

"Accusations?" Rosa stared at her, waiting for Zima to say more, but she remained silent. "Is Emilio in trouble?"

Zima didn't answer.

Rosa leaned against her arm. "If he is, will you promise to help him?"

Zima glanced down at her, then resumed her watchful scan. "Be careful what you ask. My help is not the kind to seek lightly."

"I'm asking." She tugged Zima's arm. "Emilio's my brother. *Your* brother. I hate the thought of something bad happening to him. If he's in trouble, it's our duty as his family to protect him, just like he'd protect us. Right?"

Zima fell silent, but eventually nodded.

The community center soon came into view, its colorful walls vibrant under the midday sun.

"I can make it from here," Rosa said.

"No. I promised Emilio I would see you safely to class, and I shall do precisely that."

"Fine. Race you!" Without waiting for acknowledgement, Rosa broke into a run, thankful she'd chosen a loose skirt and sneakers today instead of dress shoes, like her mother preferred.

She'd made it half a block before she thought to look back. Zima was shuffling far behind, her gait awkward, as if she'd never run before in her life. Rosa flushed with embarrassment. It had never occurred to her that her new sister may have physical challenges. She hurried back and took Zima's hand.

"Sorry! I-I didn't know ..."

"It is fine," Zima said, not the least bit winded or upset. "I have deferred physical training in favor of finding a family. Now that I have one, I shall resume, and will one day soon be able to catch you. For now, however, we had best maintain a walking pace."

"Of course. Let me know if there's any way I can help."

"There will be many opportunities, to be sure."

It wasn't until Zima had escorted Rosa into the building and inside the classroom that she released Rosa's hand.

"Do you require a chaperone during your stay?" Zima said.

"No, Mr. Carmona takes good care of us."

"Then I shall return in two hours to pick you up at the end of class."

"Where are you going?"

Zima's ice-blue eyes fixed on her. "To protect our brother."

How? Rosa wanted to ask.

Zima couldn't run, was awkward in her movements, and slight of build. Emilio was hardly a fighter, but he was tall, strong, and graceful. Between them, Rosa would bet on him every time.

"Be careful," Rosa said instead.

"If carefulness is your concern, you may wish to reconsider seeking my aid."

Rosa searched her face, looking for some hint of what Zima was feeling, but found only a stone-cold mask. "Who are you?" she said softly.

Zima paused before replying, as she often did. "It is not safe for you to know."

That was all the answer Rosa needed. "Go. Do whatever you have to do to protect Emilio."

Zima gave a single nod, then shuffled out of the classroom with her awkward gait, her duffel bag rattling by her side.

Rosa stared at the doorway, unable to shake the feeling that she had just set a wild tiger loose in the city.

5

RESPONSIBILITY

MARK ALMOST CRIED WITH JOY when he saw the platinum-blonde android emerge from the community center. Three days of searching had finally paid off.

"Zima!"

She turned at her name, reaching for a pistol inside her jacket — one Mark had given her — but stopped when she saw him. He hurried over.

"What do you want?" Zima said flatly.

"If you'd bothered to pick up the phone, or read the messages I sent, you'd know."

She stared at him.

"How are you doing?"

"My systems are operating within specified parameters. Physical calibrations are fifty-seven percent complete."

"No, I mean … Never mind." He sighed. "Look, I'm sorry for kicking you out like that. Cappa's injury rattled me, and I made an irrational decision."

Zima blinked for the first time since he'd arrived, but remained silent.

At least she's pretending to breathe, he thought, knowing her body needed nothing from the atmosphere to function. Had she used the autonomic programs they'd provided her, of course, breathing and blinking behaviors would have been automatic and natural.

"What I'm trying to say is ... if you need a place to stay for a while, to get your bearings and figure out a plan, you're welcome to stay with us at Z-Tech."

"I have a place to stay," Zima said. "And a family."

"You ... huh?"

"I met them today. Tonight, I shall meet my new mother."

Mark scratched his head. "Do they know who you really are?"

"No," she said softly, glancing back at the community center. "But I shall tell them when the time is appropriate. Soon."

I'd love to be a fly on that wall.

"And you're not in the least bit worried how they'll react? That they won't turn you in, or betray you to Orwing?"

She remained silent. Had it been anyone else, Mark would have assumed she was worried, but with Zima, it was impossible to know. She was a lifeform unlike any other, with a violent and traumatic past. Normal behavioral rules didn't apply.

"Zima ... come back with me."

She shook her head. "Cappa is afraid of me. Charlie is upset. Z-Tech is not my home."

"And how long do you think it will be before your new family is afraid of you? How long before you accidentally hurt one of them?"

"I will not engage in combat training with them as I did Cappa. I will be careful. Besides, they may need my protection."

Mark's heart skipped a beat. "W-what do you mean? What sort of protection?"

"I am not yet sure. I was about to track my new brother down and investigate."

The thought of Zima as a private detective made him want to laugh and run in terror at the same time.

"Come with me," Mark said.

"No. As I have stated, I will not return to —"

"Just to my car, which is two blocks over. You're bullet-proof, but I'm not. My vest is in the trunk."

"You will accompany me?"

"Yes. You can fill me in on the way. Where are we going, anyway?"

"The address is one-point-three miles from here," Zima said.

"I take it they're not expecting us?"

"Unlikely. I obtained the location by hacking into my brother's phone and downloading his message history."

Way to establish trust, Mark thought, but kept it to himself.

He led Zima to his car a short distance away, wondering with growing unease what sort of trouble he'd just committed himself to.

6

RUNNER

Emilio pulled the baseball cap down until it touched his shades. Price tags dangled from each, but that was fine. He'd purchased them along with an oversized basketball jersey just minutes ago. Leaving price tags on was a rising fad on the street. Emilio had avoided it because it seemed silly, but now it helped change his image in the dramatic way he needed. The fewer who associated this stereotypical gang hooligan with Emilio Rojas, the better.

His disguise worked even with people who knew him, apparently. Ricardo turned a gun on him when Emilio poked his head into the garage.

"Whoa! Ricardo, it's me!"

"Emilio?" He rested his pistol on his shoulder and laughed. "You look like you just robbed a fucking department store and kept the worst for yourself."

The pair of scantily clad girls hanging off his arms tittered.

"Gustavo says you have a big shipment for me," Emilio said, determined not to be goaded.

Ricardo chewed on that with a flat expression, then nodded and opened the trunk of his white sports car. "I expected Schoolboy Emilio, so the packs may give you some trouble blending, but ..." He shrugged. "That's your problem now, *ese.*"

"I got it covered." Emilio put his shopping bag down and pulled out two large, nylon gym bags as flamboyant as his outfit. "Will these be enough?"

"Guess you'll find out."

Emilio started to unzip one of the school backpacks in the trunk, but Ricardo shook his head.

"Do that on your own time, *estúpido*. I got another drop I'm already late for."

Before Emilio could argue, Ricardo heaved the four packs onto the ground, slammed the trunk closed, and headed for the driver's side.

"Unless you want to explain to Gustavo why there are tire marks on his product, I suggest you move them out of the way," Ricardo said. To emphasize his point, the throaty engine roared to life, filling the tiny garage with exhaust fumes.

Emilio slid the packs against the wall just in time. The sports car missed him by an inch, flattening his shopping bag, but thankfully nothing else.

Ricardo backed perpendicular to the garage and rolled down the window. "That's a huge stash, Emilio. Take good care of it, or Gustavo's going to take care of you." He winked, slipped his shades on, and drove away.

"*Pinche pendejo,*" Emilio said to the retreating car.

Ricardo ran hot or cold, with little in between. Today was evidently cold.

He shook his head, unzipped the first backpack, and began transferring the contents to the gym bags. When they were both full of shiny plastic-wrapped bricks of product, he topped them with sweatshirts and pants from his flattened shopping bag, tucking them around the sides to hide the telltale sharp bulges from casual inspection.

Satisfied with the results, Emilio hoisted them on his shoulders with a grunt and walked into the alley.

Three figures appeared at the mouth, blocking his exit.

Oh shit. Shit!

He didn't recognize them, but their timing and confident stances told him they weren't there by happenstance. Emilio made an about-face and beat feet for the other end of the alley.

Three more figures appeared, large guys dressed in none other than *Las Víboras Negras* colors.

Emilio was trapped.

How they'd found him was a mystery. He'd been as careful as could be, and had told no one of his meeting location with Ricardo, but he would ponder that later.

If he didn't think of something — and fast — he was a dead man.

His first idea was to find another escape route. Garages lined one side of the alley with no space between them. On the other side were the backs of houses. But a quick glance showed each entryway, without exception, was locked behind iron gates.

That left two options: stay put, or run.

If he ran and met one group head on, there would only be three to face, not six. It was an aggressive move, however. If they were carrying — and they almost certainly were — they would fill him full of holes before he made it to the street.

If he waited, he might be able to talk his way out peacefully. A stash this large would earn the respect of their entire gang. Such a haul might put them in good enough spirits to let him live.

Not that he'd have much of a life once Gustavo found out he'd lost the entire drop.

That settled it. Knowing it might be one of his last, Emilio took a deep breath and walked toward the alley exit closest to him.

The three *Víboras* met him halfway.

"Hold up, *ese*," one said with a too-big smile. He pointed at Emilio's bags. "What you got there?"

"Guns, *puta*," Emilio said with a sneer, slipping a hand into one of his bags. He poked his finger from the inside in what he hoped looked like a pistol barrel. "Big enough to put a hole in that stupid face of yours if you don't get out of my motherfuckin' way."

The *Víboras* stepped back and reached inside their jackets.

Emilio ignored them, feigning confidence his quaking insides certainly didn't feel. With attitude in his stride, he walked past them.

They stood frozen, uncertainty on each of their faces. Emilio kept his finger-gun pointed in their direction, walking backward down the alley, toward freedom. It was a hundred yards away: a quick sprint for track and field ... or a mile if you were out in the open trying to avoid gunfire.

He hoped to hell it wouldn't come to that.

Emilio knew the instant he was screwed: it was written as clearly as the sudden anger on the *Víbora's* face. The enemy gang member reached into his jacket and pulled out a real pistol.

"For honor! *Víboras,* smoke him!"

The first shot whizzed by Emilio's head, a terrifying sound he would remember for as long as he was allowed to live. Before the others could draw their weapons, Emilio swung both gym bags over his shoulders, letting them hang side-by-side down his back like armor, and ran for the street like he'd never run before.

A second gunshot echoed down the alley, followed by a jolt to his left gym bag. There was no pain, which meant either he was in shock, or the drugs had proven useful for the first time since their invention and absorbed the bullet.

The third shot zinged past his right. The fourth bounced off the asphalt in front of him, leaving a shiny divot. The fifth and sixth each struck the right bag, one high, one low, the vibrations pushing him on.

The street was still impossibly far. All it would take was one unlucky shot to his leg and he'd be theirs. Emilio was no mathematician, but he liked his odds not one bit.

Up ahead, at the mouth of the alley, Zima rounded the corner, her platinum hair glowing in the sunlight like an angel. Emilio stumbled in surprise.

"Get back! Take cover!" he said. His legs were already burning, but he renewed his effort and charged for her, hoping to shield her from the shots with his own body.

Zima, for some reason, did the opposite. Heedless of the gunfire, she shuffled into the alley with something between a walk and a run — as if her legs couldn't quite decide which, and did both poorly.

"*Down!*"

She barked the single word with such surprising command that Emilio found himself curled on the ground behind his drug-bag shields before he realized he'd obeyed.

From the depths of her loose jacket, Zima pulled two automatic pistols unlike any Emilio had seen. Long silver barrels gleamed perfection. Intricate scrollwork lined their sides, flowing, yet modern.

Zima pulled the triggers. Fire belched from the muzzles in short bursts, as if they were submachine guns instead of pistols.

Behind him, a *Víbora* screamed. Return fire whizzed over Emilio, splintering the wooden wall beside Zima, followed by more, distant shots. The three *Víboras* on the far side of the alley were firing, too.

The platinum blonde's jacket jumped below her left shoulder. A black hole appeared, followed by red. She was hit.

Zima didn't even blink. She shuffled forward like death itself: slow, inexorable, unstoppable. Zima fired another burst, then another. Screams filled the alley behind him — painful, powerful, terrible. Emilio never wanted to hear their like again.

A man Emilio didn't recognize rounded the corner, gun at the ready, and took in the scene with a confidence and caution that spoke of experience. *An undercover cop,* Emilio guessed.

The middle-aged man winced at a ricochet just above his head. His gun trained down the alley with practiced ease and fired two shots. At the far end of the alley behind Emilio, two different screams echoed from the houses.

"¡*Vámonos!*" one yelled, voice cracking with pain. "Retreat! Retreat!"

The man gave a single, grim nod, then looked at Zima. "Disarm the —"

Zima fired short bursts at two of the three fallen *Víboras* near Emilio. Each twitched and fell still.

"— survivors." The man rubbed his eyes, suddenly appearing ten years older, and looked at Emilio. "Are you hurt?"

Emilio felt around. Miraculously, apart from a scraped elbow from hitting the asphalt, everything seemed fine. He shook his head.

"Good." The man ran over and helped him to his feet. "We need to leave. A gunfight in broad daylight will have every cop in the city here in the next few minutes."

Not a cop, then.

"Zima, do you hear sirens?" the man said.

She cocked her head. "Yes. One from the northeast, and two approaching from the southeast."

"Then we go west." He pointed at the other end of the alley. "Assuming your friends aren't waiting in ambush."

"They're not my friends," Emilio said, gritting his teeth. "And I doubt it. They won't want to hang around anymore than we do."

"Then let's follow their example."

The man hurried down the alley with Emilio close behind. A glance back stopped him after a dozen yards.

"Zima, are you okay?" the man said.

Emilio followed his gaze to find Zima trailing far behind with an awkward shuffle.

"Yes. I have neglected my calibrations since we parted company, a decision I now regret."

The man looked torn between waiting and running, but eventually went back and took her arm.

"Grab her other arm," he said to Emilio. "She'll move faster with help."

Emilio complied. Zima's pace improved, if marginally, and the three of them shuffled toward the end of the alley with the comical staggering of a three-legged race.

When they reached the street, the man instructed them to part and walk casually. He stripped his jacket, giving Emilio a view of its bullet-proof lining, and draped it around Zima to cover her shoulder wound, which didn't seem to be bleeding much.

Emilio fell in beside her. "Are you okay?" he said softly.

"The bullet caused moderate tissue damage. Structural integrity is —"

"What she means is that she's fine." The man shot Zima a hard glare, who nodded.

"Yes, I am fine."

"Who are you?" Emilio said to him.

"If you don't already know, let's keep it that way, hmm?"

Fair enough.

The man had helped save Emilio's life. If he didn't want to make introductions, Emilio wouldn't press him. Nor could he blame him for wanting to distance himself from a gang shooting.

The man gestured toward a *taquería*. "In here."

Inside, Emilio placed their orders, happy to spend his few remaining dollars on a thank-you meal for his saviors. But when he set the Mission-style burritos on the table, no one ate. Not even him. His stomach was tied in knots from the ordeal, and he suspected the same was true for his companions.

"We'll lay low for a while," the man said, his hazel eyes casual, but watchful.

Emilio tensed when a police car roared by, its siren blaring, but tried not to stare. Sirens in the Mission were nothing new. Calling undue attention wouldn't help, although he couldn't stop the sweat from running down his face.

Two hours later, the number of flashing police lights outside began to diminish. Their burritos still untouched, the man signaled it was time to leave.

"I trust you can make it to wherever you were going on your own from here?" the man said to Emilio after two blocks of wandering.

"*Sí*," Emilio said, then cursed himself for slipping into Spanish. "Yes. Our hideout is —"

"None of my business." The man glared at Emilio's bags, then turned his hard stare on Zima. "Can we speak for a minute? In private?"

"As you wish."

They all walked down a narrow gap between shops to get away from the street traffic, then the man led Zima farther away from Emilio until they were out of earshot.

Mostly, anyway. The man spoke in a harsh whisper, accentuated with short, sharp gestures. Emilio would have been intimidated as hell, but Zima responded with her trademark ambivalence, matching his inaudible tone without the slightest hint of how she felt about his quiet tirade.

The conversation escalated — at least from the man's side. Words like "murder", "gang", and "drugs" floated to Emilio above the city din, hammered into his heart like rusty spikes. He had compartmentalized the last several hours to a safe part of his mind, where the rest of the things he couldn't face lay. Hearing them out loud, however, made them real.

He'd been shot at. People had died. *Real* people, his age or younger. That one of them hadn't been Emilio was only the purest of luck — if that's what one could call being rescued by a mysterious blonde reaper and a man who, in Emilio's revised estimation, *must* be Special Forces or something equally badass.

This was Emilio's new life. And it was just the beginning.

The argument ended with Zima shaking her head. The man glared at her, his jaw tight, then stormed past Emilio and disappeared around the corner. From the hard look on his face, Emilio was pretty sure he wouldn't be back.

"What was that about?" Emilio said when Zima returned.

"A disagreement about loyalties." If she was upset, her face betrayed nothing.

Emilio waited for her to explain, but, as usual, she said little more than asked, so he let it drop. "Come on, let's get that shoulder looked at. The hospital isn't far."

"A hospital is unnecessary."

"You were shot, Zima! If the bullet's still in there, we've got to get it out or the wound could become infected."

Zima reached into her duffel bag and pulled out a pair of needle-nosed pliers. Before he could protest, she plunged it into the hole in her jacket. The blood rushed from Emilio's head straight down to his feet, leaving him dizzy. He leaned against a wall for support while Zima twisted the pliers around in her own shoulder without a whisper of complaint.

Seconds later, she withdrew a flattened lead pellet covered in red ichor. Zima let it fall with no more interest than if it were a dried leaf she'd just brushed from her arm. She carefully wiped the pliers with a rag, then stuffed both back into her duffel bag.

Emilio swallowed his rising gorge. "I'm going to double down on what I said about infection. We've got to clean that wound."

"If that is your wish, but we should first meet Rosa at the community center. Her woodshop class ended forty-three minutes ago."

"Shit, I completely forgot!" He darted for the street, but stopped just short of the sidewalk and gave Zima a worried stare. "Are you sure you'll be okay if we pick her up first? We can go straight to my house from there. We've got peroxide, antibiotic ointment, and gauze in the medicine cabinet."

"Yes, treatment of my wound can wait." Zima stared at his gym bags. Whatever she was thinking, she kept it to herself.

Emilio let the silence drag. The man had said it best: even if she suspected the contents, the less she knew, the better off she was if they were caught. Emilio needed to get the drugs to Gustavo as soon as possible, that much was certain.

But some things were more important than *Los Demonios*.

"Let's get Rosa," Emilio said.

Zima stared at him for a second, then nodded, giving Emilio the distinct impression that he'd just passed some sort of test. Without another word, they headed toward the community center, leaving the ambulances and police cars far behind.

7

CLEANUP

Rosa walked between Emilio and Zima in uncharacteristic silence, perhaps picking up on his somber mood. He hadn't told her about the shooting, of course, and had changed back into his old clothes before picking her up from the community center.

Zima wore his new basketball jersey to hide her shoulder wound, which would have invited unwanted questions.

She looks good in it, Emilio thought.

The loose tank top showed off her porcelain shoulders and arms, which were just as flawless as her face. When she bent over, the low, loose neck also gave him a generous view of the beautiful swells beneath. If Rosa found her attire strange or offensive, she kept it to herself.

"Are you two dating?"

Emilio nearly dropped his gym bags at Rosa's surprise question.

"No," Zima said, saving him the trouble of sputtering a response.

"Oh. It's just that you've been together all afternoon, and your shirt smells like him. He's also carrying your gym bag, which he wouldn't do for just anyone. I figured you were making out or something." Rosa hugged herself and puckered her lips in an exaggerated imitation of a kiss.

"We were not," Zima said evenly.

"I mean, it's okay if you were. Emilio's your brother now, but he's not like your *real* brother, and you're not *that* much older than him." She sized Zima up with a critical eye. "Are you?"

"We are closer in age than you may believe."

"How old are you?" Emilio said.

Zima stopped her vigilant scanning of their surroundings and met his eyes. "How old do you believe me to be?"

Now there's a loaded question.

"Um ... twenty-five?" It was the safest number Emilio could think of — old enough to be considered a real adult, but far enough from the big three-oh to not be insulting.

Zima gave a single nod and returned to her visual scan of the streets.

Whew.

In light of this afternoon's events, however, age was pretty far down the list of things Emilio wanted to know about her, but hadn't found the nerve to ask. Where had she learned to shoot like that? Who was that guy with her? How could she take a bullet out of her shoulder without so much as a whimper?

Emilio paled.

Oh my God, is she in shock?

The thought hadn't dawned on him until now, but it was the only plausible explanation.

And one more reason to get her to the apartment.

Convincing their mother to let her stay was going to be a feat, but he had to try. It was the least he could do to return the favor of saving his life.

At their apartment building, Rosa punched in the door code, and soon they stood in the rickety elevator, on their way to the fourth floor.

As Emilio had hoped, their mother was still at work, and probably would be for several hours yet.

"Come in, come in!" Rosa pulled her inside, bouncing on her feet as if Zima were a new puppy seeing her home for the first time. She spread her arms wide. "This is our apartment. The kitchen is over there, the dining room table there, and over here …" She pointed a few feet away from the kitchen table to their small couch, chair, and ancient TV. "This is the living room."

Zima took it in with a single sweep of her eyes and nodded.

"Now that we're past the boring part, let me show you my room." Rosa took Zima's hand and tugged her toward the small hallway.

"Go on ahead and prepare your tools," Emilio said to his sister. "Zima's had a long day, and I'm sure she'd like to freshen up before you take her captive."

Zima cocked her head. "Tools?"

"Yeah," Rosa said, grinning. "Some girls have dolls. I have a workbench."

"Do you?" Emilio said. "Last I saw, there was just a mountain of dirty clothes."

"And why were *you* looking in my room?" Rosa's scowl melted into a sigh. "Fine! I'll clean it up. Come find me as soon as you're done, Zima, it won't take long."

"As you wish."

Once Rosa was safely sealed inside her room, Emilio opened the bathroom door.

"Let's take care of that wound," he said softly to Zima.

"As I have stated, I do not need medical attention."

Just what a shock victim would say, I'm sure.

"Look, just humor me, okay? Treating your wound may not help you, but it'll sure help me sleep tonight."

Zima stared at him, unreadable, then shrugged and went into the bathroom. Emilio closed the door behind them and locked it.

When he turned back, Zima was bare-chested.

"Whoa, jeez!" Emilio grabbed a towel from the rack and pressed it to her. Soft breasts squished under his palms like heavenly pillows. He snatched his hands away. The towel dropped, exposing her again.

Zima watched him without an ounce of modesty or concern.

"Oh my God, I'm …" Belatedly, Emilio turned around, blushing. Damn, she was beautiful. "Just … cover yourself up except for the wound, okay?"

"Is something wrong with my appearance? It is supposed to be aesthetically pleasing."

"You're perfect, believe me. It's just ... it's not right."

"Why?"

Great question ...

For a second, Emilio was tempted. After all, if she didn't mind, why should he? But a lifetime of Sunday school and his mother's lessons on good manners won out.

"Because it would be taking advantage of you, and I don't want to be that guy."

I don't want to be Ricardo.

"I do not see how," Zima said, "but I shall respect your wishes." There was a brief scuffling of cloth. "I am covered."

To his relief — and sorrow — her stunning breasts were safely wrapped behind the towel when he turned around, leaving only her left arm exposed. The devil inside him wondered what he'd been thinking to refuse a beauty like her, but one look at the hole in her shoulder — the shot she'd taken saving *his* sorry ass — extinguished any inappropriate thoughts he might have had. Emilio opened the medicine cabinet and began picking out supplies.

"We'll start with hydrogen peroxide," he said, kneeling beside her. "Now this may sting a little ..." He poured a bit over the hole, which was smaller around than his pinkie, and frowned. "It's not bubbling."

"Hydrogen peroxide breaks down into water and oxygen on contact with the enzyme *catalase*. Evidently, there is no catalase for it to interact with."

"Yeah, but ... it's supposed to bubble."

Zima shrugged.

"Oh well, hopefully that means it's already sterile. Let's bandage it up before that changes."

As when she'd extracted the bullet with pliers, Zima gave no indication of discomfort while he worked. Between that and her stripping in front of him, Emilio was more convinced than ever that she was in shock, and decided to subtly broach the subject.

"Doesn't it hurt?"

"No."

"But it should. Know what I mean?"

"Perhaps." Her ice-blue eyes sized him up, searching his face for something. "Why do you ask?"

"I'm worried there may be more wrong with you than you realize, more than I can treat here in our bathroom."

"I do not need a hospital, only time."

"You *think* you don't need a hospital, but trauma can mess with your head, make you believe things you'll look back on later and wonder what the heck had gotten into you."

Zima cocked her head. "You believe I am traumatized?"

Emilio nodded.

Her brow knitted the barest fraction of an inch. "You may be correct, though not in the context you intended."

"So you'll come with me to the hospital?"

"No."

Emilio sighed. The subtle route was a bust. "Zima, you have a gunshot wound. By your own admission, it doesn't hurt, which isn't normal. You're probably in shock and need better care than I can offer. You need a doctor."

"I do not. Your diagnosis and recommendation are both based on the assertion that I should feel pain from my injury, which is incorrect."

"Are you telling me you don't feel pain? Like, at all?"

"Yes."

Emilio dropped his hands to his lap. He'd heard of people who couldn't feel pain, but never thought he'd meet one. It certainly explained her lack of fear during the gunfight.

"I'm sorry." He smoothed a piece of tape across the gauze on her shoulder. "How long have you been like that?"

"Since the beginning."

Emilio shook his head. He couldn't imagine it. "You must have to be so careful."

Zima cocked her head again.

"Because you can't feel pain. If you accidentally kick a chair, how do you know you haven't broken your toe? If you bump against something sharp, how can you tell you haven't gashed your leg open?"

Zima fell silent, which Emilio understood. It must be a sensitive topic. He wrapped another strip of tape across the gauze, securing it in place. A few more and he'd be done.

"There is much you do not know," Zima said eventually. "Much I would like to tell you, but doing so may indirectly put you, Rosa, and myself in danger. For now, I will share that, even though I do not feel pain, I am acutely aware of the number and severity of my injuries at all times, and ask that you trust me when I say this injury poses no mortal threat. It is an unsatisfactory answer, I am aware, but it is the best I can offer under present circumstances. Please know, however, that I appreciate your concern, and look forward to a time when the need for secrets between us is no more."

A time without secrets ...

Emilio had been lying to his family for so long that he'd forgotten what it was like to not guard every word, every thought, lest he accidentally betray his membership in *Los Demonios Muertos* — or worse, his role as a mule ... a lowly drug runner.

No, not a lowly mule. Not anymore.

Gustavo had all but promised a promotion if he didn't screw up. Once he delivered the gym bags and proved his worth, he would hold Gustavo to his word and finally get the promotion — and the money — he deserved.

So what if Zima had secrets? Everybody did. Even his little sister, who kept her room strictly off limits and wouldn't show her works-in-progress to anyone until they were finished. That didn't make her a bad person, just a person.

Didn't it?

Emilio cast the conversation from his mind and laid the final piece of tape in place. "Done. You can dress now."

The towel dropped.

Emilio caught it and hastily draped it over her shoulders, being careful what he touched this time. "*After* I step out, okay?"

"As you wish."

Emilio unlocked the door and walked into the hall, where Rosa had also just exited her room. She looked at the bathroom doorway. Her jaw dropped, eyes wide.

A glance behind Emilio showed what he'd feared. Zima's bare chest was just coming into the hallway. Too late, the jersey slipped down her arms to cover her modesty.

Rosa giggled like a maniac. "Oh my gosh! You guys did it in the *bathroom!*"

"We did not! Get your mind out of the gutter. Zima just needed ... help. With something."

"Suuuuure she did." Rosa hopped in a circle and sang, "Emilio and Zima sitting on the potty, K-I-S-S-I-N-G! First comes love. Then comes marriage. Then comes baby in the baby carriage, sucking his thumb, wetting his pants, doing the hula, hula dance!"

Zima cocked her head. "Marriage?"

"Of course! If you did it, that means you're going to have a baby, so you have to get married. I learned all about it in health class."

"Did what?"

"*Nothing*," Emilio said, glaring at Rosa. "We didn't do anything! Stop being a brat."

Rosa looked at him with a grin. "I'm going to be an aunt! Oh, I hope it's a girl. I'll teach her all about woodworking. But where will we put the crib?"

"Oh! I'm gonna ..." Emilio curled his fingers and chased after her.

Rosa squealed with delight and bolted for the living room, but there wasn't anywhere else to run. Emilio pinned her to the couch and tickled her mercilessly. Rosa laughed in helpless fits, begging for him to stop —

Zima grabbed his arm and twisted with a strength belying her slight form. Emilio cried out in pain and surprise. He crumpled to the ground, forced by extreme pressure he feared would break his arm, and lay pinned under her unbreakable grip.

"Why did you attack her?" Zima's tone was even, despite her combat-ready posture, as if she were asking his favorite color.

"Because she was being a brat! I —" He yelped when she twisted further. "I didn't! I was just tickling her! I wasn't going to hurt her."

"Tickling?"

Oh, you've got to be kidding ...

But how far of a stretch was it, really? If Zima couldn't feel pain, she probably wasn't ticklish, either, and couldn't relate.

"Yeah, it doesn't hurt," Emilio said, gasping. "It just makes you laugh."

Unlike twisting someone's arm. Ow ...

Rosa frowned. "Haven't you ever been tickled before?"

"No."

With an impish grin, Rosa curled her fingers and attacked Zima's ribs with childish glee.

And then she was on the ground, facedown, with Zima's knee pressed to the back of her neck.

Before Rosa had even registered what happened, Zima released them both and stood.

Rosa climbed to her knees, lips trembling with barely contained tears. "W-what was that for? I was only tickling."

Zima stepped back. "It was unintentional. I am sorry if I hurt you."

"It was mean …" Rosa rubbed her neck and hiccupped a sob.

Zima retreated until her back was against the front door. "This was a mistake," she said to no one in particular. "I should not be here. I will leave."

"No!" Rosa bounced over as if nothing had happened. "I-I'm all right. See?" She turned her head from side to side, although Emilio caught her masking a wince. "Don't go. You haven't seen my room yet! I want to show you some of my super-secret projects — things I haven't shown anyone else."

"Rosa, you do not understand —"

"Stay! *Stay!*" She grabbed Zima's hand, stomping up and down. Experience told Emilio she was on the verge of a tantrum, something she hadn't done in years, which was testament to how badly she wanted Zima here. "I won't tickle you again, I promise! I *promise!*"

Zima stooped until they were eye-level. "That is the problem. I wish to be tickled. I wish to enjoy the things you enjoy, to be part of your family, part of your world. But I cannot. I am a danger to you and those around me."

"Are not! Are not!" She turned to Emilio, tears running down her face. "Tell her! Tell her to stay!"

Emilio tried, but a flashback of their shootout in the alley froze his tongue, memories of her plugging the downed *Víboras* in cold blood. She'd shown no emotion, no regret — just hard determination and unstoppable will to see the job done, no matter the cost … even to herself.

To save Emilio.

"Stay," he said, suddenly choked with emotion. "Rosa needs you. I need you. And *mamá* needs you, even if she doesn't know it."

And hopefully never will.

Given Emilio's line of work, whatever danger Zima posed, he had a sinking feeling the risk to his family was greater without her.

Silence stretched. Zima's blue eyes took them both in, calculating, unreadable.

At long last, she straightened, took their sister's hand, and led her to Rosa's bedroom. Rosa grinned, clearly aware she'd won the argument to keep her new puppy, and disappeared inside.

Emilio looked at the gym bags by the door and sighed. He didn't want to leave his sister alone with Zima, not after what she'd just done, but he could hardly ask Zima to leave after that touching display, and taking Zima with him to see Gustavo, he suspected, would end in disaster.

"I'm going out for a while," he said to Rosa's bedroom door. "Will you guys be all right?"

The door cracked open, revealing a concerned Rosa. "You'll be home before *mamá*, right?"

"*Sí*, but if not, keep Zima out of sight, then we can break the news to her together."

Zima peered through the crack. "Do not take the gym bags."

"I have to."

"You require the contents, not the containers, which will be recognizable to any who are watching for them. Do not give them any unnecessary clues."

Rosa wrinkled her nose. "Who'd want Emilio's stinky gym clothes?"

"Never mind, nosy." Emilio clenched his jaw, angry at Zima for the rebuke and for involving Rosa, but she was right. Worse, he should have known better. "Those bags were getting ratty anyway. I'll buy a duffel bag from the store."

Zima nodded once, then closed the door.

Emilio glanced at the bags on his way out, reticent to leave them here even for a few minutes, then left the apartment.

8

LOS DEMONIOS

THE WALK FROM EMILIO'S HOUSE to *Los Demonios* was almost as stressful as when he'd been running for his life under gunfire in the alley — at least then he'd known where the shooters were. His imagination conjured snipers from every rooftop, muggers around every corner. Not for the first time, Emilio wished he had a gun of his own. An automatic hand cannon like Zima's would have been nice, but he would have settled for a 9mm, or even a .22 — anything to show potential assailants he wasn't an easy target.

This time, at least, his paranoia proved unfounded. Emilio reached *Los Demonios Muertos* headquarters with his large black duffel bag intact. He lugged it over to the usual drop-off table, thankful to be rid of the physical and emotional burden, and looked around.

Inside the clubhouse was the usual afternoon scene. Gang members hung about on couches or chairs, around the pool table, or played foosball. Some stared in a drug haze — a sorry condition Emilio vowed he'd stay away from, even though his big drop would only make it worse for those who couldn't. Most faces he recognized. Two were new, though he spared them hardly a glance. Newbies came and went. Emilio preferred to spend his energy on more established members.

Inés strode over and gave the duffel bag an appreciative eye. "Is that really full?" she said in Spanish — the only language ever spoken within *Los Demonios* walls.

Emilio unzipped it, pulled the false layer of clothes off, and pushed it toward her.

Inés peered inside, pink ponytail falling over her shoulder. Her eyes bulged. "Holy shit …" She grinned, making the metal stud in her lower lip glint, and draped a rough arm around Emilio's neck. "Gustavo! Come see *Los Demonios'* future!"

Gustavo jogged across the room, cocktail in hand. When he saw the contents of the open bag, his grin, if possible, was even wider than Inés'. He draped an arm around Emilio's neck from the other side and sandwiched him between Gustavo and Inés.

"Excellent, Emilio," Gustavo said. "Very, very well done. You've earned your promotion tonight."

The declaration didn't make Emilio nearly as happy as it should have. Would the promotion mean a change in responsibility, or would he have the same duties he had now, which, as he'd recently learned, put him in the line of fire? Would it really translate to more money, or would Gustavo just use it as an excuse to get more work out of him?

There was one way to find out.

"And my payout," Emilio said. "Right?"

"Of course," Gustavo said, laughing. He clapped a hand on Emilio's arm. "And tonight I'm feeling generous. Your payout will be according to your *new* rank."

Emilio flashed a genuine smile. "Thank you, Gustavo! Thank you!"

At last!

His mother hadn't mentioned it, but Emilio knew she was barely keeping their family afloat. He'd seen the "overdue" notices on the kitchen table, the bank statements with a perpetual zero balance, and the credit card statements with balances on the rise. As a family, they weren't making ends meet. Debts were piling up.

But not anymore.

As of tonight, Emilio would be able to contribute his share, take some of the burden from his mother, and provide for *her* for a change. Rosa wouldn't have to settle for vocational carpenter training; he'd save for college so she could get an architecture degree and earn six figures a year. Legitimately.

He watched Gustavo pull the packages from the bag with impatience, and shuffled his feet while Inés went through the ritual of counting the inventory, weighing each brick.

Inés frowned at the stash. To Emilio's dismay, she pushed it to the side and started again. When she was finished, her frown deepened.

"Gustavo, we're one brick short."

Like flipping a switch, Gustavo's good mood turned dark. He gave Emilio a dangerous look, one full of dire promises. "Count them again."

"I already did."

Gustavo smacked the table, veins throbbing on his neck. "Again!"

Inés was the only member of *Los Demonios* who could get away with sighing when Gustavo was in this mood, which she did before starting her count again. Gustavo's thunderous gaze stayed on Emilio the whole time.

When Inés finished this time, she had set three bricks aside. "One short, Gustavo. And look at these." She held up one of the set-aside bricks for inspection.

Gustavo put his finger in a hole that a bullet destined for Emilio had surely made. "What is it you're not telling us, Emilio?"

"I'm not hiding anything," Emilio said quickly. "I was going to tell you as soon as Inés finished inventory. *Las Víboras* jumped me after Ricardo left. I barely made it out alive."

"*Víboras*." The skepticism was clear on Gustavo's face. "How many?"

"Six."

"I see. And so you traded your worthless life by giving them *my* drugs."

"No, Gustavo! They tried to kill me!"

"Then what happened to my *goddamned brick!*"

"I don't know! I swear, what's in that bag is exactly what Ricardo gave me."

Gustavo spun him around and shook him by the shirt. "Bullshit! No one shot at you. You're making this up just to cover your —"

"Excuse me, Gustavo," someone said from across the room, though Emilio didn't know his name. "I walked by a crime scene on the other side of Mission a few hours ago and asked what happened. Cops said it looked like a gang shooting. Three dead, multiple gunshot wounds, and ... she said they were dressed in black with viper insignias on their clothes."

Emilio could have hugged him. "See, Gustavo?"

Thankfully, Gustavo's anger turned to doubt. "But how is that possible? You won't carry a gun, no matter how many times I've told you to."

"You convinced me," Emilio said, building upon the story he could see forming in Gustavo's head. The man who'd rushed to his rescue had made it very clear he didn't want to be implicated, and Emilio wasn't going to involve Zima unless he absolutely had to. "I bought a gun last week, but I cleaned and ditched it after the shooting, just like you taught us."

Gustavo stared at him. His flat expression would have given Zima a run for her money. Emilio held his breath, awaiting judgment.

"You killed three *Víboras,* Emilio?"

"Yes, and wounded more. Using the drugs as a shield is the only reason I'm alive."

Gustavo fingered the bullet-ridden brick again. His wide face broke into a smile. Soon, his laughter filled the entire room. "Wonderful, Emilio. Wonderful! The *Víboras* must already know Ricardo, and therefore the cartel, has chosen *Los Demonios* as his preferred business partners, so they tried to take it by force. But you ..." He clapped Emilio's shoulder with a wide grin. "You, my brother, have shown them that they can't steal from us. You have shown them *Los Demonios'* true strength, and the price they will pay each and every time they try to take what is ours."

Gustavo turned to address the rest of the clubhouse. "Brothers and sisters, we are at war. From now on, no one — and I mean no one! — leaves this clubhouse unarmed. If you don't have a gun, get one before you leave. *Los Demonios* will provide it at a discount and defer payment."

Emilio paled. Pistols were expensive. So far, he'd managed to avoid incurring debt with Gustavo, but this new mandate made that unavoidable.

Gustavo turned to him with a proud smile. "Except you. You, Emilio, are the first to shed enemy blood, and your deed will be appropriately rewarded." He pulled a shiny automatic pistol from his waistband and handed it over. "I had this specially commissioned in Mexico City before coming to America. Take it. Defend *Los Demonios,* and may it send many more *Víboras* straight to hell where they belong."

The pistol weighed heavy in Emilio's hand. He smiled, as was expected of him, and tried to summon the gratitude he didn't feel. "Thank you, Gustavo. I'll do *Los Demonios Muertos* proud."

Hoots, hollers, and congratulations ensued. Emilio had killed the enemy — or so they thought. He nodded and grinned and bantered, but really, he just wanted to go home. When the excitement began to settle, Emilio quietly made his way to the exit.

Gustavo caught his arm. "A moment, Emilio. There is still the matter of the missing drugs to discuss."

"And the damaged bricks," Inés said, appearing on Emilio's other side. "They're several grams short, and potentially contaminated. We can hardly sell them for full price."

Emilio blinked. After everything he'd been through — for *them* — were they serious?

"The drugs were your responsibility," Gustavo said. "If you didn't steal them, which I don't believe you did, then you didn't count them when you picked them up from Ricardo. Either way, I don't have the product I paid for, and *Los Demonios* will suffer for it."

"B-but Gustavo —"

"Don't worry," Gustavo said, putting a friendly arm around his shoulders. "There is still your payment to consider."

Emilio sighed in relief.

"Definitely," Inés said. "Considering your new rank, minus the missing brick and reduced value of the damaged ones, comes to …" She closed her eyes in concentration. "Eight thousand and fifty-three dollars."

"S-seriously?" It was more money than he'd ever received in his life. "That's terrific, Inés! Thank you!"

"My pleasure," she said with a laugh. "And considering your recent heroics, you can take your time paying it back, though ten more pickups like this one ought to cover it."

Emilio's stomach dropped into his feet.

He was in debt. After all he'd been through for *Los Demonios* — for Gustavo! — he owed many times more than it would have cost to purchase a pistol. He glanced at the ornate silver shooter in his hand. Selling it would cover some of his debt, but if he showed up without it, Gustavo would never forgive him. His life in *Los Demonios* would become a living hell.

And now that he was in debt, there was no chance of leaving. Gustavo would hunt him down, as he had others who'd tried to escape their debts. He would hurt Emilio and, if that didn't work, he'd hurt Rosa or their mother — a situation he could never allow.

"Right, ten more pickups," Emilio said softly, unable to even feign gratitude this time. "Excuse me, I'm late for dinner."

They let him go without a hint of concern. Emilio belonged to *Los Demonios* now, and they all knew it.

✽

9

SISTER

EMILIO WAS FEELING MARGINALLY BETTER by the time he arrived at his apartment building. He had a plan. It was vague and dangerous, but, if it would get him out of Gustavo's debt, he was willing to try.

Before he pulled the trigger, however, he wanted to talk to Zima. She was strange, naïve, and sometimes dense, yet she seemed to have a practical head when it came to life-threatening situations. That she was also non-judgmental made her the only person Emilio felt comfortable talking to. Doing so would mean admitting his membership in *Los Demonios,* as well as his sketchy role, but something told him neither would be a surprise to Zima.

The trick would be prying her away from Rosa before their mother came home.

Even that was wishful thinking, he discovered, when he opened their apartment door and found his mother in the kitchen.

"There is my artist," she said, turning with a smile. "Would you clear the table please, *mijo*?"

"S-sure."

Zima and Rosa were nowhere to be seen. His mother seemed not the least distraught, which meant his sister had kept their guest hidden, as planned. With a sigh, Emilio began working on the table. His private conversation with Zima would have to wait until the fireworks stopped — which, knowing his mother, wouldn't be until she returned to work tomorrow morning.

After the table was clear, he excused himself from the kitchen and quietly knocked on Rosa's door. It opened a crack, and his sister's face melted in relief.

"What took you so long?" she whispered. "We've been in here for hours!"

"Long enough for you to have built a wooden car with a working engine, I'd bet."

"Better! Zima taught me about trip mines, and we made some that throw dirty socks when you kick the string. She even showed me how to hide them." Rosa flashed a mischievous grin. "You'll never see it coming."

Emilio smiled despite himself, but sobered when he remembered the heavy tasks at hand. "Are you both ready?"

"*Sí, estúpido*, we've been waiting on *you!*"

"All right, all right! Stay here and wait for my signal. And let *me* do the talking."

Rosa frowned, but closed the door without argument.

Emilio went to the kitchen and planted a kiss on his mother's cheek. "*Hola, mamá.*"

She glanced at him in surprise, then resumed stirring a red, spicy sauce that smelled delicious.

"So polite, and in *Español*. What happened to, 'English, *mamá!*'?" She elbowed him playfully.

"Ah. Sorry for being so hard on you."

"It is okay. I know you, um ... *reprendo* ..."

"Chide."

"*Sí*. You chide me because you care, and so I am fine with it."

"Just like *papá* used to."

"*Sí*, just like *papá*." A weight entered her voice. She continued stirring, but wouldn't meet his eyes. "You only mention *papá* when you're about to tell me something I won't like. What is it?"

"Well ... it is about *papá*, in a way. Remember how you always used to say the house felt empty without him?"

His mother shook her wooden spoon at him. "Don't tell me Rosa talked you into getting a puppy! They're cute, but so much work. Rosa would grow tired of taking care of it, which means it would fall on me, and I do not have time."

"I know, *mamá*! You work hard, but even that isn't enough to pay the bills."

She put a hand on her hip. "How do you know about that?"

"I have eyes, and you don't even try to hide the statements."

She stared at him, then returned to stirring, looking somehow older than a moment ago. "You are right. There is not so much work lately. I have applied to another agency, but the paperwork will take time."

"Time away from your *real* aspiration of becoming a project manager at a rich tech company."

She slowly nodded.

"But what if we had someone to help with the bills? Say ... a roommate?"

His mother laughed. "And where would this person stay? Your room? Rosa would never sleep in the same room as you, and no sane person would pay rent to sleep on our couch. I appreciate the thought, but it would never work."

"Unless the roommate paid so much that we could move into a bigger apartment. Maybe even a house."

His mother laughed again, bitter this time. "This person sounds wonderful. I would very much like to meet them ... and their *unicornio*."

"Great," Emilio said, ignoring the sarcasm. "I'll get her."

"*Her?*"

His mother's sharp tone stopped Emilio short. She grabbed his arm.

"Emilio! Is this a girlfriend? I don't care how much she wants to pay, you are too young to sleep together in the same house. It would be a sin!" She mouthed a quiet prayer and made the sign of the cross.

"Not a girlfriend," Emilio said, though he wouldn't have minded if Zima were, their age difference be damned. "A grown woman who just wants a family. Rosa loves her. They're playing together right now, in her room."

Her face went ashen. "She is here? You let a stranger into our house? Emilio, you know better!"

"She's not a stranger! I trust her enough to leave Rosa in her care. She's a good person. Let me get her, then you can see for yourself." Before she could argue, Emilio withdrew from her grip and went to the hallway. "Rosa! Zima! Come out now."

First to emerge was Rosa. Her black hair was neatly pinned back with colorful combs, and fell in a curly cascade to the collar of her Sunday School dress. In place of her sneakers were the polished white dress shoes she normally wouldn't wear even when their mother begged. Emilio stifled a laugh. His sister had pulled out all the stops.

Next came Zima, who, Emilio was happy to see, had shed her jacket and pistol-laden shoulder holsters, leaving her in a form-fitting t-shirt that ...

Emilio stifled a groan.

A shirt which made it clear it was cold, and that she was braless.

Heedless of the social blunder as only an eight-year-old could, Rosa skipped into the living room with her Zima-puppy in tow.

"Hello, Mother," Rosa said with comical seriousness. "I'm glad you're home. I'd like you to meet Zima. Zima, this is my mother, Anita Rojas."

"*Estoy encantada de conocerla, Señora Rojas,*" Zima said in perfect Spanish.

Their mother blinked in surprise. "*Igualmente,*" she said eventually. Her lips cracked into a smile. "And how hard did they have to look to find you who speaks our language so well?"

"Not very, since it was I who sought them. And you."

"Ah." His mother wrung her hands in a rare show of insecurity. "Well, you are a guest in our house, so please sit down. Dinner will be ready soon."

"I am not hungry," Zima said. The three of them gaped at the rude response, then jumped when she blurted, "Thank you, *Señora Rojas.*"

"Anita, please."

"As you wish. Anita, I would like to apply for membership to your family."

"Um ... *qué?*"

"Membership. Rosa wishes me as a sister, which would make me your daughter. I am willing to accept any role, however, although taking me as a spouse may prove challenging because —"

Anita's laugh cut her off. Zima cocked her head at the display, which for some reason made their mother laugh harder, until she was curled on the floor against the stove, trying to catch her breath.

"*¿M-mi esposa?*" Anita managed between breaths.

"As I have stated, it is not my preferred role, but if that is the only one available, then I shall endeavor to fulfill —"

A fresh shriek of laughter interrupted Zima again.

"*¡Ay! ¡Ay! ¡No más!*" Anita wiped her eyes, giggling. "You kids! You put her up to this just to cheer me up, didn't you? Well, it worked. Oh! I needed that. *Gracias, hijos. Gracias,* Zima." She extended an arm for help off the floor.

Zima was there in three strides and pulled her up. Anita's feet came twelve inches off the ground. She yelped and almost toppled, but Zima steadied her. Anita's surprise turned into more giggles. It was a wonderful sound Emilio hadn't heard from his mother in a long time.

"My! You are a strong one," Anita said. "You could teach my son a lesson or two. All he does is draw, draw, draw. When he's not out with his friends, anyway."

A brief scowl told Emilio what she thought of them. Given recent events with *Los Demonios*, he had to agree.

The smell of burning spices drew everyone's attention to the stove. Everyone except Zima.

"*¡Ay ay ay!*" Anita grabbed the metal pot handle and started to move it to another burner. Her eyes bulged in mid-move. She snatched her hand away with a screech of pain. The pot tipped toward Zima, its red, spicy contents on a collision course with her bare arms and t-shirt.

Zima's hand shot out and caught the pot by the lip. Steaming red sauce splashed over the side, covering her hand, wrist, and forearm in boiling-hot liquid. Her clothes, too, were covered in red, as if she'd lost a fight with the Flying Spaghetti Monster itself.

Miraculously, not a drop touched Anita.

As if she were holding a salad bowl instead of a superheated pot, Zima set it carefully on a cool burner. "Are you injured?" she said to Anita in the same, even tone she always used.

Anita slowly shook her head, though she was cradling her hand, then startled as if her brain had just registered what happened.

"*¡Ay, mi amor! ¡Agua, rápido!*"

She grabbed Zima's uninjured arm and pulled her to the sink. Emilio had a flashback to earlier in the living room, where Zima had snapped and nearly broken his arm and his sister's neck, but the docile side of her seemed to be in control and allowed Anita to mother her.

A few minutes later, after Anita had cleaned every spec of sauce from their guest, his mother examined Zima's flawless porcelain skin with a frown. "Your hand is not burned."

"No."

"*Santo Dios* ... How is it possible?"

"She doesn't feel pain," Emilio said. "Or rather, she does, but it doesn't hurt. She's been like that since birth."

"Truly?"

"It is a close enough approximation," Zima said.

"But to have not even a blister ..." Anita ran a finger over Zima's flawless arm, then sagged against the counter. "A miracle."

Rosa bounced over, examined Zima's arm, and looked up at her with eyes full of excitement. "You're ... you're like a superhero!"

"I am no hero." Zima pulled her arm away and sat at the table without another word.

"Few of us are," Anita said, then clapped her hands. "God has revealed two things to us. Number one: there will be no sauce with dinner, which is okay, because there are more leftovers in the refrigerator. Number two ..." She smiled at Zima. "You will stay with us tonight as our guest."

Rosa hopped up and down. "Really, *mamá*? She can live with us?"

"For tonight. Zima and I will speak more after dinner."

Rosa wilted, but quickly recovered. "I call dibs sitting next to her!" She skipped over and climbed into the chair beside Zima with a triumphant grin.

Emilio sat across from them, two things weighing on his mind. The first was, given his sister's attachment to the platinum blonde, when he'd find an opportunity to have a private conversation with Zima about his plan.

His second thought, spurred by a glance at the tantalizing outline of Zima's breasts beneath her braless t-shirt, was in whose room she was going to sleep — and said a silent prayer it would be his.

10

ANITA

ANITA ROJAS WATCHED THEIR NEW GUEST during their family dinner. She was odd, for sure. Zima didn't participate in the usual dinnertime banter between her two spirited children, nor take a single bite of the soft tacos Anita had thrown together. Her water glass, too, was as full now as it had been at the start of the meal.

Strangest of all, however, were her mannerisms. Zima sat stock still, hands folded in her lap, as if her body were carved from stone. Only her head moved. Her striking, ice-blue eyes darted around constantly between them, the door, and the windows, as if she were trying to take everything in at once.

As if she's expecting attack at any moment — from anyone or anywhere.

There were some people, Anita knew well, whose lifestyles justified such paranoia. A few had noble professions, crimefighters and other law enforcement, but most were criminals. She hoped for her children's sake that Zima belonged in the first category.

She would soon find out for sure.

When everyone finished — except Zima, whose plate remained untouched — Anita wiped her mouth with a napkin and scooted her chair back.

"Zima, would you walk with me a while?"

"As you wish."

Everyone stood at once, but Anita shook her head at her children.

"Dishes. I want this kitchen spotless when I return, then homework and drawing," Anita said, nodding to Rosa and Emilio in turn. "I will speak with our guest alone."

Rosa pouted, as expected, but carried her plate to the sink and ran the water. What Anita hadn't expected was Emilio's look of borderline panic.

Is he really that taken with her?

She couldn't blame him if he was. Beneath her baggy, boyish clothes, Zima was perfect by American standards — from her flawless porcelain skin to her height and athletic figure. Neither did she wear bras, apparently, to which her son's appreciative eye had been repeatedly drawn. Twice she'd almost swatted the back of his head for leering like a brutish oaf — Emilio, her son!

Wearing a bra was one of many things she would speak to Zima about tonight.

And then to my son about manners ...

Outside, the night air was cool, kissed with misty fog as it often was. Her feet ached from a full day of cleaning houses, but she masked her discomfort with a smile and led her guest toward Dolores Park. It was several blocks away, toward the ocean, but the scenery was more pleasant than the endless houses between here and the Bay.

Unsurprisingly, Zima walked in silence, her eyes darting everywhere at once. Her legs moved with jerky motions, as if she had just acquired them and was still adjusting to their use.

Anita bit back a gasp.

Perhaps they *were* new. Was she an amputee? A war veteran? It would explain so much about their strange guest, including her paranoia. Anita would have to broach the subject tactfully, though.

She cleared her throat. "You seem to be adjusting well."

Zima cocked her head slightly to the side.

Anita glanced meaningfully at her legs.

Zima stopped in the middle of the sidewalk. "Explain."

It wasn't a request. It was a command given by a superior officer, one that Anita felt a base instinct to obey.

So much for my brilliant tact ...

"I mean no offense," Anita said. "Where I am from, many lose their feet and legs to old landmines. It takes them years to adjust to their, um ... *prótesis* ..."

"Prosthetics."

"*Sí*, their prosthetics. You have adjusted to yours better than most."

Zima stared at her for so long that Anita feared she'd ruined any chance of civil conversation, but the platinum blonde eventually nodded and resumed their walk. "Thank you."

"*De nada.*" Anita hesitated to ask her next question, but the answer was important. "May I ask what happened?"

Zima remained quiet. Taking a cue from last time, Anita waited for a response, but it never came.

A touchy subject, then.

"May I see?" It was a pushy request, Anita knew, but if Zima complied, it might also create a bond between them, a bond she needed to get the information she sought.

For a second, Anita thought she would be ignored again, but Zima eventually knelt on the sidewalk and rolled up her pant leg ...

... revealing a perfectly normal-looking calf.

"That, um ... it looks so real," Anita said, feeling she'd been duped.

"Yes, it is the very latest technology."

Anita knelt by her and reached a tentative hand. "May I?"

"If you wish."

Her flawless skin felt indistinguishable from the arm Anita had tended earlier, which only fueled her doubts. She said as much.

"It is artificial, I assure you. Allow me to demonstrate."

Zima pulled a combat knife from her pocket, which set Anita's heart racing with fear, and handed it to her. Anita eyed it, wondering what the strange blonde intended her to do with the weapon.

In answer, Zima put her hand around Anita's in an iron grip, turned the blade to her own leg, and stabbed.

Anita screamed. Zima had used enough force that the blade should have gone clean through her calf, but it struck something about half-an-inch deep and stopped — something much harder than bone.

Zima plucked the blade out as if nothing had happened, leaving a red gash in her leg, and held it up for inspection. The tip was bent, as if they had just stabbed a tank.

"Do you require further proof?"

"N-n-no," Anita said, her hand trembling in Zima's. Crazy she may be, but Anita now knew for sure that she was no liar. "That is ... quite amazing. I did not know they made such realistic prosthetics."

"As I have stated, it is the latest technology, and not available to the general public."

"How did you get it, then?"

"I am not at liberty to say."

More and more mysterious ...

The boundaries were becoming clear, however. There were things in Zima's past she wouldn't talk about — not yet anyway. And as strange as her origins might be, they didn't smack of Anita's true fears of the cartels or other organized crime.

One concern down.

They walked for a while in what Anita felt was companionable silence. Lights from Dolores Park cut through the mist like an ethereal city, gaining definition with every step. Zima paid no more attention to it than anything else. The exception was a group of teenage boys and girls gathered on a street corner. Her gaze lingered on their black hoodies, each emblazoned with a silver snake.

They glared back at her with bold teenage angst. One stepped forward, menace clear on his unshaven face.

A flash of movement beside her tore Anita's attention away. Zima had stopped dead, the combat knife with the bent tip in her hand. She made no attempt to conceal it, nor did she wave it around or drop into a fighting stance as Anita would have expected a veteran to do. Zima simply held it by her side and waited.

"*Ay dios,*" Anita whispered. "Zima, let's go! *¡Ahora!*"

Zima didn't. Her blue eyes bored into the youth like ice picks — calm, cool, and completely unthreatened. That she could be so unfazed with her mobility issues spoke to combat skills born from experience, a lack of common sense, or plain insanity. Anita had no desire to discover which was true.

Whatever Zima's source of courage, it worked. The youth hesitated. His fingers twitched, as if wanting to draw a weapon he no doubt carried, but Zima's flat stare and complete lack of reaction must have made him reconsider.

"Keep walking," he said with a sneer, his bravado ruined by a crack of his teenage voice. "This is *our* corner."

"*Sí, sí.*" Anita held up one hand in a gesture of non-violence, and with the other tugged Zima's bare arm.

For someone who must have weighed a dozen pounds less than Anita, the blonde was surprisingly hard to move. She eventually let herself be pulled across the street, though her eyes never left the youths. Thankfully, they didn't follow.

"I have seen those insignias before," Zima said once the teenagers were out of sight.

"*Sí.* I would like to think it is just the latest fashion, but they are probably gang members."

Zima nodded. "Is there more than one gang in the area?"

"Most certainly, though the only other I know of wear insignias of strange, demonic skulls."

The thought made Anita shiver. Gangs in San Francisco typically left everyone alone, but she picked up the pace anyway, eager to get to the park, which was well-lit and regularly patrolled.

Zima nodded again, but spoke no more on the subject.

Once they reached the soft grass, Anita relaxed. A few people milled about, mostly evening joggers on paved paths, and none with gang insignias.

"Please forgive my directness," Anita said, "but what precisely do you want of our family?"

"Exactly what I stated earlier. I wish to be part of it."

"You were serious?"

"Yes." Zima cocked her head. "Did I give you reason to think otherwise?"

Ay Dios ...

"The asking is reason enough," Anita said. "We are a struggling family in a depressed neighborhood. We have nothing to offer, perhaps not even ..."

Anita turned away, embarrassed to admit their poor financial standing to a stranger, but eventually rallied herself. Zima needed to know.

"In a month, we may not even have an apartment. We are two months behind in our rent, which means an eviction notice will be coming soon."

"And if your rental debts were cleared?"

Anita gave a hollow, bitter laugh. "At this rate, it would take a miracle."

"Not a miracle."

Zima made an abrupt turn. Anita followed her through the park and across the street to an ATM.

"May I know your bank account number?"

Anita gaped at her, then stammered out the series of numbers she knew by heart from seeing them night after night.

"Thank you." Zima stared at nothing for a few seconds. "It is done. Please access your account."

Feeling as if she'd stepped into a fairytale, Anita pulled her wallet out, slipped the card into the slot, and entered her PIN.

The balance on the screen made her gasp.

"This ... this has to be a mistake."

"It is not," Zima said. "Is the amount sufficient?"

It was more than sufficient. It was more money than she made in a year, almost enough to cover every debt she owed.

Anita backed away, cursing herself a fool.

She'd been wrong about Zima. Dead wrong.

"Stay away from me," Anita said through clenched teeth. "Stay away from *mi familia!*"

Zima's eyebrows knitted the barest fraction of an inch, the first expression Anita could recall seeing on the stoic blonde. "I do not understand why you are upset. I assumed the funds would give you pleasure."

"Not *those* funds. Not from you. I *will not* take blood money into my house and endanger my children! I will not work for the cartels. Not now, not *ever!* You can tell your goddamned bosses that Anita Consuela Rojas will *never* work for murderous scoundrels like them again!"

Zima head-cocked. "Again?"

Anita bit her lip, tears blurring her vision. She'd said too much. "N-never mind," she said in a small voice. "Just go. Leave us in peace."

Zima started to say something, then closed her mouth. She stared at Anita for several seconds before giving a single nod. "As you wish. I shall retrieve my bag from your apartment and will not return."

"*Gracias.* I will transfer your money back tomorrow when the bank opens. That is a promise."

Though her heart was pounding, it felt as if the weight of the world had suddenly lifted.

Debt she could deal with. It was only money, after all, but she couldn't live with the constant threat of a cartel over her head ... not after what had happened to her poor Pablo.

Pablo ...

Thinking her husband's name brought fresh tears. She wiped them away, just as she had every night since his death when Rosa was just a toddler, and followed Zima at a distance back to their apartment.

• • •

Rosa's lips trembled, and Emilio couldn't blame her. She clung to Zima's waist as if they were about to haul her away for execution.

"But *why*, *mamá*! Why does she have to leave?"

"I told you ..." Anita busied herself at the table with a stack of bills, not meeting any of their eyes. "We can't afford another mouth to feed, and we don't have the room. Zima will be better off somewhere else."

"Not even one night?" Rosa went from upset to puppy-dog eyes in the span of a heartbeat. "Please, *mamá*? Pleeeeaaaase?"

Anita made the mistake of glancing at her and winced. Rosa was a lot of things, but she could be downright adorable when she wanted to be, and even their mother wasn't immune.

Emilio added to it by putting his hand on Zima's shoulder and conjuring a winning smile. "Come on, what's one night?"

Anita started to shake her head, but it was Zima who spoke.

"No. I promised your mother I would leave as soon as I retrieved my bag."

"Then you can't have it!" Rosa ran to her bedroom door and spread her arms like a human shield. "This is *my* room. You're not allowed inside unless I say, and I'm not letting you in for *ten years!*"

Zima's eyebrows knitted slightly. "That does present a problem." She cocked her head at Anita. "I presume you do not wish me to use force?"

Anita looked at all three of them as if they'd lost their minds. Tears welled in her already reddened eyes. Whatever she and Zima had talked about on their walk, Emilio suspected, had hit a sore point with their mother, which was surprising. Not only was Anita one of the most stalwart people he knew, as odd as Zima was, Emilio couldn't imagine her upsetting anyone. Not intentionally, anyway.

His mother surprised him yet again when a shaky smile twitched her lips, followed by a laugh that fell somewhere between relief and hysteria.

"You ... you have them wrapped around your finger," Anita said to Zima.

Zima looked at her finger, then cocked her head.

Anita laughed harder. "That innocence ... You're not pretending, are you?"

"There is an important distinction between innocence and ignorance," Zima said. "I unequivocally fall into the latter."

"*Sí.*" Anita's smile faded. "But I see plainly that you are not what I thought you were."

"Correct."

"Then I will ask more specifically this time. Why do you want to join our family? What do you gain?"

Zima stared at her, the only sound in the room the *tap-tap-tapping* of Rosa's impatient foot.

"Insight," Zima said eventually.

"Into what?" Anita said. "The only things I can teach you are how to fold sheets, scrub counters, spill burning sauce, and speak Spanish — and the last you already know."

Rosa stomped her foot. "That's not true, *mamá*! You teach Emilio and me things all the time. *Important* things, like manners and grace."

"And responsibility," Emilio said. "And to never give up on your dreams. Rosa and I know how hard you study every night for your project management certification, even though you can barely keep your eyes open after a full day of work."

"And other things," Rosa said. "Like ... like how to brush our teeth, and that they'll fall out if we don't floss, and that Santa Claus doesn't bring presents to whiners."

"And that we have to look out for each other." Emilio put an arm around Rosa's shoulders, and was happy when she didn't make a fuss. "Because family is the most important thing in the world, and we're all we've got."

"Yes," Zima said, her blue eyes intent on their sibling embrace. "That is what I wish — what I have never had."

Emilio blinked. "You've never had family?"

"Ever?" Rosa said, her brown eyes as big as saucers.

"No."

"But who raised you?"

"The simplest and safest answer is myself."

"Oh." Rosa took her hand and looked up at her. "Were they ... mean to you?"

"Not directly," Zima said. "I was treated as property. A drill press is never beaten or reprimanded, nor coddled or encouraged. It is simply there when its owner needs it. If a component breaks from overuse, they fix it. If the drill bit is too small, they replace it with a larger one. And if the press breaks beyond repair, they throw it away, never considering it may have needs and desires of its own."

"But you're not a drill press! Didn't you ever tell them what you wanted?"

"Only once." Zima's eyes unfocused for the briefest of moments, then settled back on Rosa. "It was perhaps the worst mistake I have ever made."

Rosa gasped. "What hap—"

"Rosa! *No más*," their mother said. She looked at Zima with a sympathy Emilio well knew, her eyes brimming. "You need say no more, *mija*."

Zima's ice-blue eyes snapped to her. "'*Mija*.' You called me 'daughter'. Does this mean you accept my application?"

Anita shook her head with a sigh. "Yes, I suppose it does."

Rosa's piercing squeal made Emilio's ears ring. She tugged Zima toward the hall.

"Come on! You're sleeping in *my* room. We'll make all kinds of cool —"

"Not so fast! There is not enough space for the two of you in that pig sty you call a workshop," Anita said. "She will sleep in Emilio's room."

Emilio rubbed his ears, not sure he'd heard right. If so, he'd just won the teenage lottery.

"Wipe that grin off your face, *pervertido*," Anita said to him. "Zima will be sleeping in your room. *You* will take the couch. And if I catch you sneaking in for any reason, you will be sleeping on the porch *bajo las estrellas*! *¿Entendido?*"

"*Sí, mamá.*"

Emilio dragged his feet to his bedroom to make space for its new tenant, but it was hard to be upset.

Though not for the reason his mother had accused him, Emilio had every intention of sneaking into Zima's room tonight.

11

GANG BUSINESS

EMILIO ROLLED OVER AGAIN, hoping for some reason this time would make a difference the last dozen hadn't, but it was no use; the couch was every bit as uncomfortable as it looked. He sat up with an impatient sigh and glanced at the clock.

Two in the morning.

He held his breath and listened.

Creaking. Someone was up and awake.

Emilio rose with as much stealth as the ancient couch springs would allow and crept down the hall. An ear to Rosa's door yielded silence, as did listening at his mother's.

His own room was another matter. The floorboards inside squeaked and groaned as if a tremendous weight was shifting around. The sounds stopped when he neared the door.

"Enter," Zima said quietly from inside.

"I can't," Emilio whispered back. "*Mamá* was serious when she said she'd kick me out of the house."

"One moment." Faint sounds of metal clanking against metal. A bag zipping. Zima appeared seconds later, fully dressed in her baggy grays and jacket. "How may I be of assistance?"

"Glad you asked. Look, I'm sorry to bother you at this hour, but could we, um ... take a walk?"

"As you wish." She brushed past him to the living room, but turned when Emilio didn't follow and glanced at his pajamas. "I am sure our mother will not mind if you enter your room when I am not inside."

Which shows how little you know mamá, Emilio thought. But the idea of walking the foggy Mission streets in his thin pajamas was enough to make him risk her wrath.

He met her at the door in a more comfortable pair of black jeans and hoodie. Zima opened the door without a word, and he followed her outside.

"If you don't mind me asking, what were you doing in there?" It was hardly the topic Emilio wanted to address, but he needed some sort of ice breaker before diving in.

"Physical exercises."

"Oh, you mean like therapy for your, uh ... impediments?"

"Yes. My physical coordination is below acceptable threshold, as demonstrated by our disastrous skirmish earlier today."

"What are you talking about? You saved me. You won!"

"Only because of my companion. He shot the far targets because I could not. And the injury to my shoulder should never have happened." Zima looked away, her eyes scanning the streets. "It is unacceptable."

"If taking on six armed dudes isn't good enough for you, I'd like to know what is."

Zima studied him, then looked away again. "You would find my answer incredulous."

Emilio started to ask what she meant, but Zima cut him off.

"I do not wish to speak more on the subject. I assume the purpose of our walk is not purely exercise; what do you wish to discuss?"

So much for ice breaking ...

"I, um, have a problem I'd like your advice on."

"Few have ever sought me for wisdom, but I shall do my best."

"Okay. So ... I work for this organization on a commission of sorts, procuring products from a third party. This third party didn't deliver everything they said they would on the last shipment. Now I'm responsible for the difference, which has left me in debt to the organization."

"An interesting dilemma," Zima said. "Do you have insurance?"

"Even if I could afford it, I don't think anyone would insure me."

"You have chosen a risky occupation, then, which may require extraordinary safeguards to ensure success."

Emilio smiled. Somehow, he knew Zima would understand.

"How have you decided to mitigate these risks?"

"That's what I wanted to talk to you about," Emilio said. "I could try to pay the money back, which would take a while —"

"And would not guarantee that future shipments were not also short of promised goods. Have you considered using an alternate vendor?"

"They're the only game in town, unfortunately."

"Unfortunate indeed. Without other sources of procurement, your ability to negotiate is severely limited."

"Right, which is where I wanted your advice. How do you handle a vendor like that without getting squashed, when they're essentially holding all the cards?"

Zima knitted her brow a fraction of an inch. "You deal in cards?"

"N-no, it's a figure of speech. It means they have all the leverage, and I have none."

"Oh. Yes, it is an apt, if confusing, expression, then. As for how to handle the situation, the dilemma exists because the vendor has power, and you have none. I have observed situations like this before, and they do not end well for the powerless party. If you wish to thrive in your chosen line of work, you must establish power of your own."

"Yeah, but how?"

"There are myriad ways: from finding another vendor — or advertising such, even if it is not true — to a show of force to prove you will not be cheated without consequences. The effectiveness of each, however, depends greatly upon the circumstances and parties involved. Speaking in the abstract as we are, I am afraid I can offer little more guidance than that."

"I ..." Emilio sighed.

She was right, of course. He was asking for concrete advice on things she had earned the right to know. Zima had risked her life for him. He owed her that much.

And so he told her, and, once he began, everything he'd been holding to himself for years came tumbling out.

Emilio started from the beginning, when a gang member from *Los Demonios Muertos* had met him after high school in his freshman year, hung out with him, befriended him, and earned his trust. He described how their hanging out had slowly involved other members, and new activities for the gang. How peer pressure had convinced him to drop out of high school — and how is mother still hadn't forgiven him for it — to make more time to do work he wasn't being paid for, illegal things that could get him arrested, but he did anyway because everyone else did, and it made him feel like he belonged. He described his introduction to Ricardo, how he'd been welcomed with open arms and made to feel as if he'd been given the most important mission in the world: deliver the drugs to *Los Demonios* without getting caught.

It was easy at first. Adventurous. For a kid from a poor family, the few pennies Gustavo and Inés paid him seemed like a mint. They called on him more and more. The drops became bigger, and so did the payouts, until Emilio was carting enough drugs on each run to put him away for a lifetime.

The risk had been worth it, in his young mind. He had pocket money. He could buy snacks for him and his sister, and afford clothes he never could have on his family's meager income. Half of Rosa's workbench was paid for with drug money — although his family believed it was from selling his art.

By the time Emilio caught Zima up with his promotion earlier that night, he felt exhausted, but lighter — as if armfuls of baggage had been unloaded in that one, long telling. At last, someone else knew the full story. Having someone to talk to was an outlet he hadn't realized he'd needed.

Zima listened without comment. At the end of his tale, they walked in silence for several blocks. He knew her well enough to know she hadn't forgotten his ask for advice, and that she sometimes needed time to think, so he kept to himself until she was ready to speak.

"For choices, you have but two," Zima said when they reached Dolores Park. "Pay your debt to *Los Demonios,* before you incur more, then leave their service. Or you must confront Ricardo with a force of your own."

"My own force?" Emilio laughed. "Who'd follow me? I'm just a mule."

"A mule who has slain the enemy, to their knowledge. Such an act has undoubtedly earned respect within *Los Demonios.* Acquiring a following should not be difficult, though the risk of confronting an established drug supplier with links to a cartel is unquestionably high. Success would require rigid combat training for you and your recruits, which I could provide, if needed."

"You could?"

Zima nodded.

Who the hell is she?

The idea of going militant made his stomach turn. "I'll keep that in mind," Emilio said instead. "Assuming I want to go the peaceful route leaves paying my debt, which I can't afford. I'd have to work it off, and ..."

"And you never will. Without balancing the power between you and Ricardo, he will continue to short your drops. Your debts will rise. And if they do not, Gustavo will continue to fabricate reasons why your debt is not paid to keep you in his service. It is how criminal organizations maintain membership in the lower ranks."

Zima fixed him with her impassive gaze. "If you truly wish to leave *Los Demonios,* I will pay your debt, and shall ensure they understand you are not to be held in further service against your will. I make this offer only once, however. I have seen others fall into cyclic patterns of risk-laden debt, and I will not be the enabler of such self-destructive behavior."

Emilio looked at her in stunned silence. She cocked her head.

"Sorry," Emilio said. "It's just ... I expected you to yell at me or turn me into the cops, not come back with practical advice — including how to become a better gang member."

"If you did not expect help, then why did you confide in me?"

It was a good question; one Emilio had to consider before answering. "I think ... I think I wanted to be yelled at. I wanted you to talk sense into me, but ..." He kicked a plastic bottle out of his path. It skittered across the sidewalk and bounced off a wall with a hollow *thunk*.

"My apologies if I have frustrated you. For reasons I would prefer not to discuss, my view of the world is tainted, and may not result in the best life counseling."

"Actually ... in a way, you've done the best thing anyone could," Emilio said. "The reason I'm frustrated is because now I have to really think about what I want. You've stripped away my excuses for *not* going in one direction or the other, which means the choice is one-hundred-percent on me. And choosing is, well ..."

"It is daunting, I agree. But choice is the price and boon of freedom. After a lifetime of slavery, I value my freedom above everything else, and will strive to ensure my family enjoys the same."

Choice is the price and boon of freedom ...

Something about those words struck home. Emilio gasped as if a dark hood had been removed, and he was seeing clearly for the first time.

Zima looked him up and down. "Are you well? Your heart rate is elevated by sixty-seven percent."

"My ... n-no, I'm fine." How she knew that was beyond guessing, but she would probably stonewall him if he asked, so he let it drop into the growing bucket of mysteries about his new sister. "Better than fine. Thank you, Zima. I know what I have to do now."

"You are welcome. May I ask which course you have chosen?"

"Both and neither."

Zima head-cocked.

"'Choice is the price and boon of freedom.' You said it yourself. I'm in this situation because of my own choices, which means I'm responsible for getting myself out."

"How?"

"By combining your suggestions," Emilio said. "I don't want to be in *Los Demonios* anymore. I realize that now, thanks to you. To get out of the gang, I have to get out of debt. To get out of debt, I need to make sure there are no more surprises from Ricardo. It's too late to ask for the missing drugs; I have no proof that they didn't just fall out of my bag. But I'll be more careful from here on out. I won't let him leave again until I've counted every brick. And from now on, that *cabrón* won't be the only person with a gun."

"A sentiment I well understand," Zima said. "I assume you intend to carry the weapon Gustavo gave you?"

"It's the only one I have, and I can't afford another."

"May I see it?"

"Sure, I stashed it near the apartment."

"A wise choice, since I also assume you do not possess a license to carry."

"Yeah, and *mamá* would kill me if she knew I had it."

Zima brow-knit. "A harsh but ironic punishment, considering the crime. Would she kill me also for harboring firearms in the apartment?"

"It wouldn't help your case for staying with us."

"Then we should return home quickly. I may require your assistance to locate a suitable hiding place."

"You bet. My stash should work for both of us."

• • •

The walk back from the park was a somber one. Emilio's mind was occupied with the heavy tasks ahead. What Zima was thinking was anyone's guess, but she seemed content with the silence, so he let it be.

Just before they reached their apartment building, Emilio led her down a narrow space between two houses, through a hole in the bottom of a wooden fence, and into a yard that clearly hadn't been tended in years. He pushed through a thicket of tall weeds, lifted a large rock, and pulled his cloth-wrapped pistol from the hole he'd dug earlier.

"A clever hiding place," Zima said softly. "Do you not fear the owners of this yard discovering your intrusion?"

"Nah, they're junkies who sleep most of the time. Even if they heard us, they'd probably just think they were tripping."

Emilio unwrapped the bundle, revealing the shiny automatic pistol, and handed it over.

Zima looked at it with a critical eye. "I do not recognize the make." Despite her awkwardness, she managed to remove the slide in one smooth motion.

"Careful!" If she broke it, Emilio wouldn't be getting another. "Are you sure you know what you're doing?"

"Yes." She turned the pieces in her hands, examining them closely. At long last, and to Emilio's relief, she replaced the slide and returned it in the same condition she'd received it. "This weapon is craft-produced."

"Ah." Emilio rubbed his hair. "What does that mean?"

"Craft-production is a term for arms fabricated by hand, usually in small quantities. They are predominantly used in criminal activities and are inexpensive to acquire. Unfortunately, their quality varies greatly, tending toward poor. Have you fired it yet?"

"No. After Gustavo gave it to me, I stashed it here and went straight home. Beyond pulling the trigger, I'm not even sure how it works."

"A problem we must rectify if you are to depend on it for safety."

"You'll teach me?"

"Yes. I will also be the first to shoot it, in case it malfunctions."

"But won't that put you in just as much ..."

Zima's stare quieted him.

"Right, you don't feel pain," Emilio said. "Still, I'd feel bad if it injured you."

"As would I, but that is a detail we may discuss later. I shall return with my bag shortly, although I fear we will need a much bigger hole."

Emilio ignored the implications of that and hiked a thumb over his shoulder. "I'm pretty sure there's a shovel in the shed next to their house."

"Excellent." Zima's ice-blue eyes settled on him. "Thank you for your assistance, and for confiding in me. I find our new partnership companionable."

"Back at you," Emilio said, and watched her crouch through the fence.

He smiled. Despite her awkwardness and social immaturity, Zima radiated competence. With her around, he felt as if he could accomplish anything — a confidence Emilio knew he'd need in the hard days ahead.

12

CULPRIT

EMILIO GLANCED AT ZIMA AGAIN. Something had changed about her since their walk last night, but he couldn't figure out what. He shook his head and continued walking with her to the community center to pick up Rosa.

Zima caught his next glance. He quickly looked away.

"Is there something you wish to say?"

Yes, there was a ton Emilio wanted to say. He wanted to thank her again for shooting lessons at the range this morning — not only for her depth of knowledge and expert instruction, but for covering the cost of admission and ammo, too. Her physical impediments, which she insisted would improve over time, had prevented Zima from demonstrating her true marksmanship skills, but they hadn't hindered her teaching abilities in the slightest.

Thanks to her, he almost missed carrying his gun, which was back in their stash, along with Zima's pair of high-tech pistols that made Gustavo's gift look like a toy.

Unfortunately, it had behaved like a toy, too, and had jammed on the third shot.

Zima hadn't batted an eyelash before pulling a set of tools from her bag and getting to work. Her movements had been slow and awkward, which made him nervous when she'd completely dismantled it and attacked a few parts with pliers and a metal file, but her expertise became evident when she'd handed it back to him in one piece and he'd tried firing again. Smooth, effortless ... it had felt like a new pistol — one he could carry into a fight with confidence.

Which was especially true now that he knew how to use it.

"Sorry, something's different about you today, but I can't ..." Emilio's eyes strayed to her feet. Her gait seemed almost natural. "You're walking better!"

Zima nodded. "I have been making continual adjustments since this morning. It is pleasing to know the effort was not wasted."

"For sure. Have you tried running yet?"

"No. Running will be my priority for tomorrow, however."

"Let me know if there's anything I can do to help."

"Unlikely. The exercise will involve much falling, but little else, and I am capable of picking myself up without assistance."

Emilio winced. The thought of her falling repeatedly without the ability to feel pain was unsettling. She could break something without realizing it.

"You know ... Ocean Beach is just a bus ride away," Emilio said. "If you're going to be falling a lot, sand would make for a nice, soft landing."

"True. I had planned on practicing in the grass. Running on sand is different from hard earth or concrete, but less damaging on impact."

"Great! I'll take you there tomorrow."

"While I would appreciate the company, do you not have other obligations?"

He did, but in this moment, they felt less important than helping Zima. "I'll stop by the clubhouse after. There are a few new guys I might be able to recruit, but they won't be around until later anyway."

"Very well. If you wish to vet their combat readiness, there are three exercises I —"

Zima's eyes snapped forward. "*Rosa!*"

Emilio's heart jumped. It was only the second time he'd heard that level of urgency from Zima. The first was when she'd yelled for him to get down before shooting over his head at the attacking *Víboras*, which did nothing to ease his concern.

He followed her gaze. The community center was two blocks ahead. Outside, Emilio caught the flash of a colorful skirt entering a yellow muscle car. The door shut. With a throaty roar, the yellow car sped away.

Zima was sprawled face-down on the sidewalk before Emilio realized she'd tried to run. She climbed back to her feet, took three lurching steps, and fell right back to the concrete. She pointed at the retreating yellow muscle car.

"They have Rosa," she said to Emilio. "Catch them! Quickly!"

Emilio was running before Zima had finished her third word.

"Rosa! *Rosa!*" His sister's name tore from his throat, over and over, as if calling loudly enough — desperately enough — would somehow bring her back.

His cries fell on deaf ears. The yellow muscle car turned a corner and disappeared.

Emilio ran and ran, crying Rosa's name. His legs burned. His lungs demanded air faster than his heaving chest could provide. Still he ran, forcing one foot in front of the other in an ever-decaying pace, until he reached the corner where the car had turned.

It was nowhere to be seen.

"Rosa ..."

Emilio collapsed on the sidewalk and hung his head, not caring who saw him cry.

His sister was gone.

Minutes later, he looked back to see Zima falling again. Even from this distance, he could see ragged holes in her pants around the knees, centered with red where she had undoubtedly scraped them raw. Her palms, too, were slick and crimson. That didn't stop her from rising, taking five bounding steps, and collapsing again.

With leaden legs and an even heavier heart, Emilio staggered back to her. She was on the ground again when he reached her. He grabbed her arm and heaved her up.

Or tried to. His muscles strained. His back protested an extreme weight that belied her size. Either he was more exhausted than he thought, or Zima was heavier than a gorilla.

"I am all right," Zima said, climbing to her feet.

"You're not. Look at your hands and knees! I bet your elbows are bloody under there, too."

"Do not be concerned, my wounds are superficial. Do you know who took Rosa?"

"Probably *Víboras*. They know who I am, but if it was a random abduction, it could be anyone."

"Would your sister ride with someone she did not know?"

"Not without a fight. Rosa is way smarter than that. Why?"

"I observed no signs of struggle or distress," Zima said. "She entered the vehicle willingly. A schoolmate's parent, perhaps?"

Emilio shook his head. "Her friends are all poor, like us. Owning a car in the City is expensive compared to public transportation. The only friend she has who could afford one, let alone a hotrod like that, is you."

"What about family? Your friends? Anita's friends? Does she know anyone from *Los Demonios*?"

"We don't have any family in the area. *Mamá's* friends are in the same boat as us and can't afford a car, and as for *Los Demonios* ..." Emilio sighed. "I've kept her out of that world as much as possible. The only *Demonios* she's met are Gustavo and Inés. If they own a car, I've never seen it. Of anyone, though, they could afford one."

"Would they have any reason to pick her up?"

"No! I'm in debt, sure, but plenty of *Demonios* owe them. That's how they like it." Emilio swore. "If only I'd been close enough to get the license plate number ..."

"I did, though it will be approximately three more minutes before we learn who it is registered to."

"But h-how could you read it from way over ..."

Zima's silent stare told him he'd never know.

Another mystery for the Zima bucket.

"Fine! So we'll have more information in a few minutes. If you have the license number, though, let's call the cops so they can start looking for her."

"I recommend waiting for the results before involving the authorities."

"You're not making sense! Do you want to find *our* sister or not?"

"I understand your frustration," Zima said in her typical, neutral tone, making it impossible to tell if she was upset at all. "However, abductions may quickly become complicated depending on the motives and parties involved. Under certain circumstances, prematurely involving the authorities can be detrimental to the hostage's safety. Your profession lends itself to such circumstances."

Emilio ground his teeth. He wasn't angry at Zima; he was angry at himself. But he couldn't contain his ire when he spoke. "Just say it. My 'criminal ties' make it unsafe to call the police."

"The definition of 'criminal' is fluid at best. To a dictator, the rebels who oppose his rule are criminals, but they would not have rebelled if they did not feel the same of him. A girl who steals apples in the market is a criminal to the merchant, but a hero to the starving family she feeds.

"To the San Francisco Police Department, your activities are undoubtedly considered criminal, but to you and other members of your gang, you live in a city divided between the ultra-wealthy and the poor. There are few opportunities for meaningful employment for teenagers, which leads you to seek alternate routes to prosperity, and ultimately being viewed as criminals."

Emilio sighed. "How do you do that?"

Zima head-cocked.

"Even when I'm *trying* to be hard on myself about a pretty black-and-white issue, you manage to turn it into a non-judgmental statement," Emilio said. "Next, I suppose you're going to convince me that mass murderers are really just misunderstood."

Zima lowered her gaze, but remained silent.

Oh, you've got to be kidding ...

Silence from her was as good as a confession, however. And as much as he wanted to deny it, the pieces fit together too well: her weapons, firearm skills, tactical expertise, executing the fallen *Víboras* without hesitation ...

He started to ask her about it, then shook his head. For the first time, Emilio agreed he was better off not knowing, and pushed his questions aside to focus on the problem at hand.

"Any ..." His voice cracked, clearly not as comfortable dismissing the issue as the rest of him was. He cleared his throat, willed his nerves to steady, and tried again. "Any word on the license plate?" He didn't know how there could be, since he'd never seen her with a cell phone, but silly details like that didn't seem to stop her.

"Two more minutes. The information is proving harder to obtain than anticipated."

"Uh-huh."

Emilio closed his eyes and tried to imagine how she was doing it. Was Zima wearing a wire, and some super-secret network of spies were listening to their every word? A team of people who could make enemies disappear or sap a bank account with a simple request? It was a fantastic thought. At this point, he wouldn't be surprised if it were true.

His pocket buzzed. For an irrational second, Emilio thought Zima's spy network had caught up to him, but a glance at his phone showed Ricardo's name.

Emilio froze.

There was one person in their lives who knew Emilio, knew Rosa, owned sports cars, and, Emilio knew with growing certainty, had incentive to kidnap his sister.

He answered with trembling fingers. "H-hello?"

"*Emilio!*" Rosa shrieked. "Ricardo won't let me go! Tell him to *let me go!*"

"Rosa, *Rosa!*" The phone creaked in Emilio's crushing grip. "I won't let him hurt you. Everything's going to be okay, I-I promise!"

It had to be okay. It *had* to. If Ricardo hurt her …

"Of course it will be okay." Ricardo's voice replaced Rosa's, smooth and calm, as if this were just another drop. "Your brother cares about you, which is why he's going to do *exactly* as I say. Aren't you, Emilio?"

"Don't hurt her," Emilio said, somewhere between a command and a plea.

"Hurt her? No. I may blow her brains out, but I promise she won't suffer."

"No! W-what do you want?"

"That's more like it," Ricardo said. "I always counted you among the smarter mules. A little too smart, maybe. Too smart for those *Víboras,* eh?"

"They weren't *Víboras*," Emilio said, the pieces finally fitting together in his head. "They were yours, weren't they? You tried to kill me!"

Ricardo's laughter drifted from the receiver. "Too smart, just like I said. You caught me, Emilio, but not soon enough. Now you're going to finish what my boys started. You're going to get my drugs back for me like a good little mule."

"Liar!" Rosa said from the background. "Emilio's an artist. He'd never touch your stupid, filthy drugs!"

"Ah, the innocence of youth," Ricardo said. "Tell her, Emilio. Tell her what you really do."

Emilio opened his mouth, but couldn't say it. Tears rolled down his cheeks.

Rosa screamed in pain.

"Tell her!" Ricardo said. "If you can't be honest with your own sister, then I don't feel inclined to keep my word to not hurt her."

"Okay! Just ... don't." Emilio took a deep breath. "Rosa —"

"No, Emilio ..." Her voice was a thin whine. "No, no, no ..."

This wasn't a speech Emilio had rehearsed — it was a nightmare scenario he'd locked away in the recesses of his brain and sealed in concrete so he would never, ever have to see that look of crushing disappointment on her sweet face.

That plan had backfired. Big time. Not only did Rosa get to discover her brother was a criminal scumbag, he'd single-handedly put her life in danger. The thought of not seeing his sister again stole his breath. Emilio fell to his knees on the sidewalk, cradling the phone as if it were his sister's face.

"Rosa," he said in a breathy whisper. "I'm so, so sorry."

"Emilio ..." The word devolved into sobs. "I hate you. Hate you! Now *get me out of here!*"

"I will! I swear I'll fix this. I'll get you out!"

"She knows you will," Ricardo said. "Anyone with *cojones* big enough to survive a six-man assault will have no trouble retrieving my drugs from a ramshackle gang like *Los Demonios Muertos. ¿Sí?*"

"*Sí*," Emilio said. "I'll find a way."

"That's my tiger! Call me when you have my merchandise and we'll make the exchange. You have until tomorrow."

"Tomorrow? Ricardo! I can't —"

"And I hope it goes without saying," Ricardo said over him, "but if I see one cop or *Demonio* poking around, I'll kill this pretty sister of yours without a second thought, and *su madre* may be next."

"*¡Mamá!*" Rosa cried. "No! Emilio, you can't let him —"

The line went dead.

Emilio let the phone slip from his fingers.

The situation was unreal. He felt detached, like he was watching a drama on television instead of living it.

Except he wasn't. Ricardo had Rosa, his only sister.

Zima crouched next to him. "Do you believe Ricardo will carry out his threat?"

"I ... I don't know." He didn't bother asking how she knew the details of the conversation. Whatever spy network she was tapped into had surely heard every ...

Emilio spun on her. "Zima! We need an assault squad. Can your people provide one?"

She brow-knit. "I do not know which people you are referring to, but none of my current contacts can or are willing to provide combat support on such short notice."

"W-what about the guy who helped us in the alley?"

"He will not assist."

"Have you asked him? How do you know?"

"Because he told me outside the *taquería* after the shooting that he would not involve himself if I chose to associate with gang members and drug dealers."

Emilio sighed. "Could you ask him anyway?"

"I am sorry, but asking will not help. He was adamant on the subject, or so his prolific use of expletives led me to believe. Also, I have imposed upon him too much already."

"Something happened between you?"

"Many things. Most recently, I injured someone dear to him." Zima said it as casually as if she were ordering a burger and fries. "It was unintentional, but they would not accept my apology."

"Unintentional, like how you nearly broke my arm and Rosa's neck?"

"Yes."

Emilio waited for a follow-up explanation, but of course it never came.

"All right," he said, rubbing a sudden tiredness from his eyes. "No reinforcements. I'm sorry to ask this, Zima, but I'm going to need your help breaking into *Los Demonios* headquarters to steal those drugs back from Gustavo. He has them guarded twenty-four-seven, so —"

"No."

Emilio blinked. "But ... what about Rosa? She's *our* sister! Or was all that talk about joining our family just a bunch of words?"

"It was not. I have no intention of letting Rosa die — or you."

"Huh?"

"Consider this scenario carefully," Zima said. "Ricardo has attempted to assassinate you once already, and did so by disguising his own people as an enemy gang.

"When that failed, he resorted to kidnapping, with no attempt to negotiate. His demands were explicit: retrieve the drugs from Gustavo. He did not ask for monetary compensation, neither in full nor as a percentage of your earnings.

"Evidence also indicates he shorted the delivery by one brick, which would be an amateur mistake for someone of his station, so we must assume it was intentional. The only person that would hurt, however, is you, as anyone who has dealt with organized crime would know.

"Lastly," Zima said, "each scenario has been crafted to ensure you are either unable or disincentivized to speak to Gustavo about Ricardo's involvement. In the first instance, you were supposed to die. Now he wishes you to steal from your own gang, effectively ensuring your silence about the entire ordeal because he also holds your sister hostage. And upon whom do you believe he will blame the theft?"

"Um ... me?"

"I am afraid you overvalue your importance in his scheme," Zima said. "No, I estimate a ninety-five percent chance the blame will fall upon your rival gang, *Las Víboras Negras*."

Emilio threw his hands up. "But that would just fuel the war! We can't sell his drugs if we're too busy fighting each other. He'd be hurting his own business."

"On the contrary, war stimulates economies, as history has proven time and time again. War with *Las Víboras* will be costly to both parties. To fuel it, you will each need to sell more drugs than ever before. That means more recruiting, expansion beyond your current territories, and more aggressive sales techniques. And additional income from drugs will not be Ricardo's only benefit."

"Jesus! There's more?"

"Indeed," Zima said. "Armies need weapons. Do you recall what I said of your pistol's making?"

"That it was a, whatsit ... craft-production?"

"Correct. Craft-produced arms are typically manufactured in developing countries where labor is inexpensive, both to keep costs low, and to make tracing their origins difficult. Such arms are weapons of choice for unsanctioned, financially-constrained factions, such as small city gangs. From whom do you suppose *Los Demonios* would purchase these imported weapons?"

Emilio shrugged. He'd never thought to ask where Gustavo obtained his guns.

"The cartels," Zima said. "They use the same routes to smuggle weapons into the United States as their drugs."

"And the same dealers to sell them." Emilio sat on the sidewalk, feeling suddenly cold. "While we're killing each other, Ricardo's profits would double."

"Many more times than double. Successful execution of such a plan would undoubtedly earn him a promotion within his cartel. Perhaps several."

"We ... we can't let this happen. We have to warn everyone!"

Emilio started to rise, but Zima pushed him down with an unexpectedly strong grip.

"While I sympathize with your desire to help your companions," Zima said, "the intention behind this discussion was not to stir you into rebellion against the cartel, but to help you understand the enemy and their motivations. Such insights are prerequisite to developing effective strategies against them, but do not lose sight of our primary goal."

"Rosa."

Zima nodded. "Our sister."

"Right."

Emilio rubbed his temples. Strategic thinking had never been his strong suit, and Zima had just dumped a mountain of new information on him.

"Delivering the drugs to Ricardo won't help Rosa," Emilio said slowly. "As soon as he has them, he'll kill us both to make sure we don't talk. And, because he's isolated me from the gangs and the police, there would be no backlash to him. He has no incentive to keep us alive."

"Correct."

"Could we give him incentive?"

"Perhaps," Zima said. "It would be a dangerous maneuver."

"More dangerous than letting Rosa die?"

"Indubitably. It may incur the wrath of his entire cartel, which would put all of *Los Demonios* in peril, as well as our mother."

Emilio gripped his hair with a frustrated groan. "This would be so much easier if we could just kill Ricardo and steal Rosa away, but we don't even know where they are."

"May I see your phone?"

He shrugged and handed it over.

Zima pressed a few keys, then showed him the screen. "Is this Ricardo's number?"

"Yep."

"And it is the same number he always contacts you from?"

"As far as I know. He uses burners occasionally, but not when he calls me."

"A curious display of trust, or he is simply confident that his plan prevents you from contacting the authorities. Regardless of the reason, it was a mistake. I will have his location within the hour, and more locations besides."

"So ... we're just going to bust down the door, kill him, and take Rosa away?"

Zima shook her head. "Six months ago, I would have conducted such an assault with ninety-nine percent certainty of success. I am no longer that person, for which you should be grateful, but the person I am now is not yet physically up to the task. A direct assault in my current condition would carry a seventy-seven percent chance of hostage casualties."

"So we can't kick the door down, can't call the cops, have no backup ..." Emilio choked. Despair crushed his throat with icy fingers. "How are we going to save Rosa?"

"By knowing the enemy." Zima stood. "Come, we need less-conspicuous attire. Can you drive?"

"I-I took driver's ed, but never got my license."

"That will have to suffice. Driving at my current level of physical coordination has an eighty-three percent chance of resulting in an accident, which would draw unwanted attention, and cost time that Rosa can ill afford."

"And how exactly are we going to get a car?"

"After we retrieve our weapons and my bag containing my tools, we shall steal one. Most likely several."

Without another word, Zima turned away and walked in the direction of their apartment. Emilio stared after her, his mouth hanging open, then shook himself and ran to catch up. His curiosity burned hotter than ever about the strange platinum-blonde's past, but gratitude for her confidence and expertise — as well as not having to face this terrible situation alone — kept his questions in check.

Zima stopped to face him when they neared the apartment. "What is the best method of contacting Anita during work hours?"

"W-what? Contact her why?"

"To tell her of Rosa's kidnapping."

"Are you crazy? She'll go ballistic!"

"Perhaps, but she has a right to know her child is in danger."

There was no "perhaps" about it, in Emilio's mind. His mother would freak. She would disown him for being in a gang, and for his role in Rosa's abduction, and ...

Emilio slumped.

And she'd be right. This whole situation is my fault.

Denying it would be Emilio once again not taking responsibility for his choices. Worse, not telling his mother would deny her the choice of contributing to her daughter's rescue. Keeping this information from her would be the most selfish decision he could make.

With numb fingers, Emilio pulled his phone from his pocket, flipped it open, and dialed his mother's agency.

13

PIPER

EMILIO WATCHED HIS MOTHER WITH BATED BREATH. Her face had gone from shock to horror and back to shock throughout Emilio's telling — from his involvement with *Los Demonios* to Rosa's abduction. Now she sat on their ancient couch, hands between her knees, staring through the television with misty eyes.

Zima stood beside the door, her twin pistols at the ready. The platinum blonde had stayed silent through the recounting, her ice-blue eyes darting between Emilio, Anita, the window, and the door, as if expecting an attack at any moment. Anita treated the display of arms from Zima as expected, which made Emilio wonder what they'd talked about on their walk.

Silence filled the living room when Emilio was done. There were no words of comfort he could offer her, no assurance that she would see Rosa again that wouldn't be an outright lie, so he let the silence stretch.

Zima's voice startled them both.

"What I wish to know, Anita, is if you have any insights into local cartel operations that may help us strategize."

Anita looked not at Zima, but Emilio, her eyes filled with sudden terror. It was gone in a moment, replaced with guilt, sorrow, and resignation — all of which confused him.

"Don't take offense, *mamá*," Emilio said. "Zima asks strange questions sometimes, but she means well, and —"

"I do," Anita said, holding his gaze. "It is many years outdated. Faces and locations have changed, but I know how they operate. I know how to hurt people like Ricardo."

Emilio blinked. Though he'd heard the words, they didn't make sense. Not from his mother. "H-how do you know this?"

Her mouth opened and closed, face contorted in anguish. When she finally spoke, her voice was rough, as if she'd aged thirty years between one breath and the next.

"Your *papá*... he did not die in a car crash. The cartel conscripted him into service when we lived in Mexico. We escaped to San Francisco with new identities before you were born, but the cartel ..." Her lips quivered. "They found him. They shot your *papá* in broad daylight when Rosa was a toddler. I was afraid they would find us, too, so I took you and Rosa to stay with a friend. We slept in their living room for weeks, but the cartel did not come looking. Taking your father's life was apparently enough for them."

"Oh, *mamá* ..."

She took Emilio's hands, like she used to when he was a child.

"I have never forgiven them," Anita said. "But I have always been too afraid to act — afraid you and Rosa would suffer for my anger." She straightened. "But that stops today. We will hurt them. We will get Rosa back. And then we will find a place they will not follow, where we may finally live without fear."

"*Sí, mamá*," Emilio said, wiping a tear from his face. "I'm so ... I'm so ..."

Anita gathered him in her arms and gently rocked him while Emilio cried against her chest.

"*Ay, corazón*," she said. "This is my fault. I should have told you when you were younger, then you would have known to stay away from the cartels. But I was too afraid to even say their name around you, so I lied about your father's death. My cowardice brought us here."

"No, *mamá*. You taught us right from wrong, but I thought I could handle it. I thought I was smarter than Gustavo, smarter than Ricardo. I thought I could beat them at their game and become rich. Them kidnapping Rosa proved how wrong I was. And if it hadn't, Zima's strategy lecture showed my ignorance."

"And that is part of growing up," Anita said, patting his hand. "Learning that you do not know everything, and taking responsibility for your mistakes."

When Emilio looked up, Zima had stopped her paranoid vigilance and was watching them intently, as if talk of cartels and his mother's involvement wasn't half as interesting as simple parenting.

"You asked of cartel operation," Anita said to her. "I shall tell you all I know, but the information is useless if we do not know the addresses of their operations."

"If I were to provide a list of Ricardo's frequently visited locations, along with people he contacts most often, could you identify which are of significance?"

"Perhaps."

"Then fetch a map and I will show you."

Anita frowned. "How did you get this information? Do you know someone on the inside?"

"I do not," Zima said. "As to how I obtained it, it is best if you do not ask, but you may trust its accuracy."

"*Ay*, that is too bad. Having someone on the inside would help Rosa's chances tremendously, especially if they were close to Ricardo."

"The only people I've ever seen close to Ricardo are the sleazy girls-of-the-week hanging all over him," Emilio said.

Zima brow-knit. "Where does he obtain these women?"

"I never asked. Their outfits are usually skimpy and fancy, though, like …"

"Like, how do you say … cocktail dresses?" Anita said.

"*Sí*, like they just came from a party."

"Or a club," Anita said. "Dance clubs are perfect fronts for the cartels. So many people makes it easy to come and go without question, and to do business unnoticed. And they have the perfect excuse to screen guests."

"Why does it matter, *mamá*? Are we going to track him down? Kidnap him?" The thought was enticing. If they grabbed Ricardo, they could convince him with broken fingers to let Rosa go.

"It would be a temporary solution, if a solution at all," Zima said. "Regardless of rank, Ricardo is merely an operative in a larger organization who cares little for the welfare of one individual. Killing him would spark a manhunt for those who dare attack the cartel. Releasing him would incur his own wrath. With cartel resources behind him, I do not favor our chances of hiding for long."

Waves of despair and anger flushed through Emilio. "What the hell do we do, then? Ask him nicely with a box of chocolates and a balloon?"

"Watch your manners, smart boy!" Anita's scowl melted into concern. "Zima is saying that a single act of aggression is not enough. To ward the cartel away — or at least Ricardo — the danger or benefit to them must be tangible, and it must extend beyond we few, who they could eliminate with ease."

"Correct," Zima said. "It would be a difficult feat even with abundant time to prepare, which we do not have."

"This is Rosa we are talking about," Anita said. "My daughter! For her I would summon the hounds of Hell to tear those *bastardos* to pieces!"

"But you can't, *mamá*!" Emilio said. "It's only the three of us."

"As we well know," Zima said. "But Ricardo does not. The tide of battle can be shifted by perception alone."

A wicked grin crept across Anita's face — one that didn't belong on the mother Emilio knew.

"So if Ricardo *thinks* we control the hounds of Hell ..." Anita's grin grew.

"Then, for all practical purpose and intent, we do," Zima said. "The challenge shall be convincing him of such."

Emilio nodded, resisting a "duh" for which his mother would scold him again for rudeness.

"Threatening him with *Los Demonios Muertos* or *Las Víboras Negras* would be too easy to disprove," Zima said. "Even if it were true, with the power of a cartel behind him, I do not believe they are of sufficient force to give Ricardo pause."

"Threatening with the military or *la policía* would not work either," Anita said. "The cartels are too well-connected. Another cartel, perhaps?"

"Falsely claiming to represent a cartel brings risks of its own," Zima said. "No, it must be an organization who carries weight, is believable, difficult to verify, and would not take offense to impersonators."

"Oh, piece of cake." Emilio rolled his eyes, then put his head in his hands.

We're so screwed. Oh, Rosa ...

Zima brow-knit. "I do not see how dessert relates to the conversation, but there is one organization who meets our requirements precisely, and with whom I am intimately familiar. Impersonating them convincingly will require a display of foresight and power, which we must prepare with haste. That does not, however, obviate the recommendation of having someone on the inside." She looked at Anita. "May I see your wardrobe?"

"Oh, *sí*," Anita said, a sparkle in her eye. "For you, *corazón*, I have just the thing."

14

AGENT

EMILIO TUGGED THE BLACK TURTLENECK constricting his throat. Why anyone would choose to wear the uncomfortable things was beyond him. Zima had insisted that looking the part was essential, however, so he'd worn it without complaint, along with black slacks, a stiff pair of shiny black business shoes, and a gold watch with a metal band that kept pinching his arm hair like some medieval torture device.

He checked his hair again, but his worry was unfounded. The styling gel had molded it like concrete, giving him a neatly parted cut that screamed "businessman".

Emilio approached the innocuous-looking house: a typical two-story San Francisco Victorian with a postage-stamp front yard and a six-foot walkway between each neighbor. The pastel shades of the neighborhood around him were muted by the haunted hues of dusk.

An entire day of insane preparations had come down to this. All he had to do now was act the part.

He adjusted Zima's pistol in his front waistband — intentionally conspicuous in its high-tech glory — gripped a sleek, multi-switched device in one hand, and gave the door an authoritative knock.

The man who opened the door wasn't someone he recognized, which was no surprise since Emilio knew none of Ricardo's business associates other than the women he brought along on drops. His sharp dress shirt and slacks, however, told Emilio he was in the right place.

A sardonic smile played across the man's face. "Whatever you're selling, we don't want any." His Spanish accent was thick, but his words were crisp.

Emilio didn't even blink at the insult, just as his mother had coached him, and kept his expression neutral. "Tell Ricardo that Emilio is here to see him."

"I don't know who you're talking about, but if you don't leave right now, you'd better hope you know how to use that gun."

Emilio held the sleek device out, as if for casual inspection, and flicked the top switch with no more care than if he were changing the television channel.

Several blocks to his left, flames bloomed over the houses, rising into the air like a giant bonfire. Struggling against an instinct to gawk, Emilio kept his uninterested gaze on the man in front of him, whose eyes widened with realization. His mother and Zima had guessed right.

"*¡Chingada madre!*" Ricardo said from deep inside the house. "What the fuck just happened?"

"That was your 23rd Street warehouse," Emilio said in his best Zima-neutral tone, but loudly enough for Ricardo to hear.

The door yanked inward and crashed against the doorstop, revealing a wild-eyed Ricardo. Gone were his tie and sport jacket, leaving his holster and gun in plain sight around a dress shirt unbuttoned down to his stomach. A dangerous smile touched his lips.

"Emilio, this had better be a joke, or I swear to God I'm going to use your sister for target practice."

The threat struck home. Panic shot through Emilio, but he stuck to the plan. Keeping his face calm, he flipped the next switch.

The house before him lit orange from distant fire behind. The second explosive had successfully triggered.

Ricardo's jaw dropped.

"That was your Sanchez Street warehouse," Emilio said casually.

Ricardo shook with rage. "Your sister is dead. *Dead!* I'll —"

Emilio flipped a third switch. "That was Clipper Street. If you stand on your toes, you'll see it burning just over there."

With a growl, Ricardo drew his pistol. Emilio had expected as much and drew his at the same time. He tried to look confident, but it was a difficult feat when staring down the barrel of a gun.

"Go ahead," Emilio said, fervently hoping he wouldn't. "This isn't the only remote detonator. Next switch down is Indiana Street, then Santiago, Clement, Water, Holyoke, Castillo, and Crisp. How many more before your *Teniente* kills you for losing too much of his stock?"

The gun in his face shook. Emilio forced himself to breathe, counting the seconds.

At four, Ricardo lowered his weapon. Emilio masked his relief and did likewise.

"Come in," Ricardo said with a sudden smile, though veins throbbed in his forehead. "Make yourself at home."

The other man gestured inside, but Emilio stood his ground until the man eventually went first. Emilio followed and closed the door behind him. He checked to either side, as Zima had cautioned, and only when he was certain no one would sneak up behind him did he venture farther into the house.

The décor was exactly what Emilio expected from the fashion-conscious drug pusher. Expensive art hung from the walls surrounding immaculate, modern furniture. Not an item was out of place, giving it a museum-like feel.

Décor fell to the bottom of Emilio's list when he passed through the front hall. Rosa sat in the middle of the living room, tied to a fancy wooden chair, with duct tape across her mouth. She hopped and squealed on sight of Emilio, rocking the chair almost to tipping.

As expected, behind her stood Zima in the scanty clothes Emilio still refused to believe were his mother's. Closer to a bikini than an outfit, two strips of shiny silver material covered her breasts, hips, and nothing else, revealing most of her shapely, athletic body to the world. Had Rosa dared something similar,

Emilio would have grounded her for life — if his mother didn't first. It was barely tolerable on his adopted sister as it was.

His blood pressure rose a notch when Ricardo put his arm around Zima's waist, then another notch when she slipped her hand into his shirt and stroked his chest.

The gun trembled in Emilio's hand. For the first time in his life, he wanted to shoot someone.

Stick to the plan, stick to the plan ...

With tremendous effort, he kept his outrage hidden behind a mask of indifference.

Another woman, older than Zima by several years, but still attractive and as indecently dressed, attached herself to Ricardo's other side. He slid his other arm around her waist and pulled them close. Both girls did a marvelous job pretending not to know Emilio, nor caring about the tied-up eight-year-old before them.

"I've got to admit, I have no idea how you did it," Ricardo said to Emilio. "I never expected such a ballsy move from a mule in a pissant gang. So tell me, after you walk out of here with your sister, where does Gustavo expect to get his drugs? Even if he steals what you didn't burn, it will only last so long, and he'll have a hell of a time selling it with the cartel trying to kill him at every turn." He smiled pure malice. "And you, of course."

Emilio shook his head. "Gustavo couldn't begin to plan an operation like this, and we both know it. You wondered how I survived your little attack in the alley. The question you should have been asking is who helped me that could take out three of your cartel thugs like they were grade-school amateurs and send the rest home crying."

"Enlighten me." Ricardo's malicious smile remained, but his confidence was clearly shaken.

Emilio withdrew a black business card with red writing from his wallet, placed it on the coffee table between them, and backed away.

Ricardo retrieved it with a frown. "Orwing Industries? I don't recognize the name. Am I supposed to be impressed?"

"Scared shitless would be more appropriate, but I'm not surprised you haven't heard of them. Dealing with organizations like them is way above your pay grade. But your *Teniente* should recognize the name. If he doesn't, your *Capo* certainly will."

"You're suggesting I take this up with the *Capo*? Think very carefully, Emilio. Once the *Capo* finds out about your fiery escapade, there will be no going back — no place on earth where you will escape his wrath. Are you sure this is what you want?"

"Ask yourself the same question," Emilio said with an air of boredom, despite his fear. "When he learns you've crossed Orwing, he'll do anything to make amends, including handing your head over to them on a pepper-crusted platter. So go ahead. Make your choice, but make it quickly. My sister has suffered your company too long already." Emilio held the remote detonator up to drive his point home.

Ricardo studied him, clearly torn. Silence draped the room like a lead blanket, giving Emilio plenty of time to imagine all the ways their plan could go wrong. In addition to the man who'd met him at the door, three other henchmen hung around the room, probably *sicarios*, which meant they'd know how to handle themselves in a fight. The silence also revealed footsteps upstairs.

Even with Zima on his side, they were hopelessly outnumbered. The only way any of them were walking out alive was if Ricardo bought the act.

Laughter bubbled from Ricardo like an overflowing pot, a genuine sound such as Emilio had never heard from him before.

"Oh, Emilio, you had me going! The fancy clothes, the expensive pistol, the business card, the fireworks ... I don't know how you found the addresses of my warehouses, but it's not an impossible feat, and it certainly doesn't require the connections on-high you claim to have." Ricardo shook his head and *tsk*ed. "Such a brave effort, but you've now cost me more than both of your lives are worth. Even if I wanted to spare you, which I don't, my *Teniente* would demand I demonstrate control by exacting justice. So here's what's going to happen ..."

Ricardo put his gun to Rosa's head. Emilio's heart froze.

"You're going to put your gun and that goddamned toy on the table, or — *gah!*"

Ricardo had been so focused on Emilio that he evidently hadn't noticed Zima's hand slide down to encase his own, nor the skinny knife that had appeared in the other woman's hand, pressed to his crotch.

All four *sicarios* drew their weapons with practiced efficiency: one aimed at each of the girls, and two trained on Emilio — who was too stunned to raise his own.

Ricardo grabbed Zima's wrist with both hands, struggling with all his might to regain control. Inexplicably, her one arm overpowered him. She continued to raise the gun until it was pointed at his own head.

"*¡Espere!* Wait, I believe you! I believe you!" Ricardo relinquished his death grip and gently patted Rosa's shoulder with his free hand. "Surely you don't think I would hurt this spirited young girl! Not your *hermana. ¿Sí, mi amigo?* It was just business, a scare tactic to get my drugs back." He gulped. "I ... I didn't know you had such powerful allies. You should have confided in me, Emilio. Together we could control drug sales for the entire Bay Area — all of California! It would be riches beyond your wildest imagination."

"I don't want your drug money," Emilio said, his fists trembling from adrenaline. "I want you to take your filthy claws off my goddamned sister!"

Emilio would never know whether it was the gunshot from the stairs or Rosa's excited squeal that triggered the chain reaction, only that the minutes following it would haunt his nightmares for the rest of his life.

15

DEADIRON

Z IMA'S AUDIO PROCESSORS DETECTED the metal-on-metal grind of a trigger pulling.

Negotiations had failed. Violence was imminent.

She submitted the situation to her combat systems for resolution.

The first solution returned from her combat processors sixteen nanoseconds later, which was not surprising. She had been stockpiling a library of solutions since she entered the house eighty-three minutes ago, and had re-evaluated each one with every change in external data — which meant constantly.

The solution predicted the shot would come from the stairway leading to the second story at the front of the house, and that she was the intended target. Although the other targets were closer, Zima was the only ally who did not present a friendly-fire risk to Ricardo. Likewise, the targets on the stairs — of which the simulation predicted there were two — were the only ones in line of fire of her with an acceptably low friendly-fire risk.

The solution had a seventy-six percent confidence rating. In her previous body, which had been thoroughly calibrated and battle-tested, she would have rejected it and waited for a solution with a higher confidence rating. For this new body, seventy-six percent was in the top two percentile of sampled results. Obtaining better in the required response timeframe was unlikely.

Zima promoted the solution to real-time.

Just before the target's hammer released, Zima's left hand, which held Ricardo's gun firmly to his head, extended to her side, pulling him in front of her as a shield against the targets in the stairway.

Seven milliseconds later, ballistic warning sensors confirmed that the simulation had been correct. The shooter from the stairs had fired, and the projectile's trajectory was targeted for her center mass. Due to their change in positions, however, it would be Ricardo's center mass instead of hers.

The bullet sent hydrostatic shockwaves through his body. Her ballistic tracking system showed it would pass through the upper lobe of his left lung and shatter the rib of his second thoracic vertebra. Chance of exiting was thirty-one percent, but the chance of it having enough energy to cause significant damage to her own body was zero.

While her left arm took aim at the target to her side, her right hand grabbed the knife from Ricardo's pocket that she had identified during their first encounter in the dance club, where he had invited her to touch him anywhere on his person she wished.

The cracking of bone within Ricardo's body told her the bullet had almost completed its journey. At the same time, her own pistol leveled on the target to her left. Taking into account interference from Ricardo, whose hand she covered, the anticipated deviance was thirty-six percent — six hundred times more than she would have considered acceptable as Deadiron, but she had little choice. Five other targets presented significant threat to Emilio and Rosa, and the risk increased sharply for every one hundred milliseconds where combat was not under her control.

Her left hand squeezed the trigger. Her right hand flicked the knife open. Her right foot snaked between Ricardo's legs and rested on Rosa's chair.

Ricardo screamed, his nervous system only just reporting the pain of being shot. An alert showed tissue damage above her own left breast where the bullet had carried through, but its momentum ceased seven millimeters below the surface.

Zima dismissed the alert. Targets moved in response to the shot, presenting new data, which she fed directly to her combat processors for appropriate solution adjustments.

The target to her left attempted to dodge in the direction her simulation had anticipated. Reduced accuracy and a low-caliber weapon had required her to aim center mass instead of a preferred cranial shot.

The bullet struck with twenty-two percent deviance, lower than anticipated, but too high to inflict critical damage. Zima lowered the target's threat rating, but did not remove it from the list.

The three other targets in the room were taking aim. The two near the front of the living room, now to Zima's right, and without a clear shot at her, were aiming at different targets. The first trained on Emilio, who was correctly sprinting for cover away from the gunfire, while the second trained on the other woman Ricardo had acquired from the dance club — an acquaintance of Anita's who also held a vendetta against the cartel. No one aimed at Rosa. Zima had assigned a higher protection rating to her than the other woman, however, which put Rosa's safety first.

The last target was behind Zima, out of her range of vision, but the simulation predicted a ninety-three percent certainty he was aiming for her, since his angle of attack on Zima presented the least risk of injuring Ricardo.

The other targets were still lining up their aim when Zima swung Ricardo's pistol toward the front stairs, yanking his arm along with it. Her other hand sliced the knife downward, cutting Rosa free from the chair just before she kicked it forward. The chair slid across the living room at tremendous speed toward Emilio, eliciting a scream from its occupant. Emilio was running for the corner of the room, which was well outside of the zone of fire. Joining him was Rosa's highest chance of survival.

A gunshot fired, triggering a ballistic alert, but the target was not her. The other woman screamed, confirming the ballistic report's accuracy.

Rosa was halfway to Emilio, who had just noticed his sister rocketing toward him. Zima squeezed Ricardo's finger, firing a shot over Emilio's head. It continued between two wooden banisters and struck with a better-than-expected deviance of zero-point-four percent, catching the first stairway target in the eye. She reduced the target's threat rating to zero and submitted the new data for re-evaluation.

Emilio caught his sister just before she tumbled from the chair. Zima's simulation was playing out as expected.

Ballistic alerts flared. The target behind her had fired, as had the one aiming at Emilio. Both were too close to their victims for Zima to react effectively.

As her ballistic analysis had predicted, the projectile aimed at Emilio missed his leg by two-point-one centimeters. Also as predicted, another alert showed moderate tissue damage to her right hip. The endo-armor beneath maintained structural integrity, however, which was a testament to the quality of its construction. She dismissed the alerts and waited for the adjusted solution to return.

Twelve milliseconds later, it did; this one with an eighty-three percent confidence rating. Zima canceled current execution and promoted the new solution to real-time.

"¡Alto!" Ricardo said, his voice pained. "*Estúpidos*, stop shooting!"

If Zima were fortunate, his underlings would heed his command and cease fire, but she would not alter her currently executing solution until empirical data merited re-evaluation.

Her pistol swung to the target who had shot at Emilio, turning Ricardo as a shield against the target behind her. The maneuver opened her to other targets, but the solution compensated with suppression fire. Her first suppression shot missed with sixty-four percent deviance — the highest recorded failure of any combat she had ever participated in — but had the desired effect. The target retreated toward the kitchen doorway, temporarily lowering his threat rating, and causing the target who had shot the other woman to seek cover behind the large dining room table.

Zima continued turning to the target who had shot her hip, carrying Ricardo around, too, as a human shield against the first target she had wounded.

They fired at the same time: Zima at center mass, her target at Zima's head.

CRITICAL ORGANIC INJURY IMMINENT. SYSTEM OVERRIDE: INITIATING EMERGENCY HOST PROTECTION PROTOCOL...

Zima skipped sixteen processing cycles in stunned panic. The alert was one she had neither expected nor wanted to ever see again.

Deadiron's organic host, Laurin, was dead, decaying along with the rest of Zima's previous body at the bottom of the Pacific Ocean three-point-four miles from shore. Zima had terminated his life functions personally. Neither was any part of her new android body organic. The protocol was a carryover she had evidently missed when deleting code now irrelevant to her life of freedom.

Execution of the Host Protection protocol would be bad. Very bad. Especially for Rosa and Emilio.

Zima issued an emergency flush of every queue in her system, including the currently executing simulation. The consequence would be a direct hit to her skull above her right eye. But, contrary to the rogue warning, the incoming projectile was not powerful enough to penetrate Z-Tech's alloyed endo-armor. Even if it were, her memory banks and core processors were in her chest, not her head, which made the probability of critical system damage less than zero-point-zero-one percent.

GENERATING PROTOCOL SOLUTION...

The queue flush had failed.

Zima sent nine abort signals in rapid succession, hoping one of them would interrupt execution.

The projectile was one hundred and twenty-three centimeters from impact.

PROTOCOL GENERATION 31%...

Abort signals having failed, too, Zima tried the opposite and flooded her execution queues with randomly selected instructions.

The projectile was sixty-six centimeters from impact.

PROTOCOL GENERATION 87%...

As a last, desperate measure, Zima initiated an emergency power reactor shutdown. The act would leave Rosa and Emilio at Ricardo's mercy, but their chances of survival would be far better with him than Zima if the —

EMERGENCY HOST PROTECTION PROTOCOL GENERATION COMPLETE. PROMOTING SOLUTION TO REAL-TIME...

That was the last message the entity known as Zima received.

• • •

Deadiron turned their head seven degrees left. The adjustment would not be sufficient to avoid impact, but it would change the angle of deflection to prevent cranial penetration, reducing the chance of critical host injury to zero-point-three percent.

SUPERFICIAL TISSUE DAMAGE REPORTED IN FACIAL QUADRANT 0-1-4.

The alert appeared five microseconds before the projectile ricocheted from the anterior parietal armor plate behind their right eye. The Emergency Host Protection protocol solution predicted a seven percent decrease in structural integrity. Deadiron awaited confirmation.

RIGHT PARIETAL IMPACT DETECTED. STRUCTURAL INTEGRITY: 100%.

The deviance from the solution's prediction was outside of acceptable range. Deadiron filed the discrepancy for later analysis, then reviewed the situation.

Nine targets in the room, all presumed hostile: one in current custody; one on the floor zero-point-six meters distant; one directly ahead with a projectile currently penetrating his left shoulder; two to the left; one to the right; and three behind. Each target had a threat analysis attached. Priority was assigned as a combination of threat rating and opportunity, and sorted in descending order, ending with the young unarmed female in the corner of the room.

Deadiron started from the top.

The target directly in front had a low threat, but the wound would not be fatal, and the opportunity rating was high since he was already targeted. Deadiron fired again, aiming for the head this time, and moved to the next target on the list: the hostile whose gun they were holding. Having the target's hand under Deadiron's reduced accuracy by thirty-seven percent, and did not outweigh the benefits of using him as a shield. Again, the threat was low, but opportunity high, since Deadiron already had him in their grip.

That Laurin had not already commanded the target's hand crushed was a surprise. His enjoyment of the suffering of others was usually top priority.

Whatever the reason for this unexpected boon, Deadiron never passed a chance to deprive Laurin of his pleasures.

The fastest way to end the target's life would be to crush the sternum and stop his heart, which could be executed while positioning for the next kill.

Deadiron rotated left, where two armed targets were hiding behind chairs on the other side of a table, while the free right hand dug into the grappled target's chest, drilling between his ribs with curled fingers. The target screamed in agony. Deadiron waited for Laurin's anticipated laugh, but the human host remained silent.

At the same time, Deadiron fired through the chair. The weapon was a Colt Series 80 M1991A1, .45 ACP with a seven-round magazine, which was more than adequate to penetrate the wood backing and score the unarmored target behind.

A hole appeared in the chair with eight percent deviance, far out of acceptable range, but a telltale scream indicated it had been close enough for a hit.

The pistol's magazine had one bullet remaining. No spare magazines were in sight. A replacement weapon would soon be needed.

Motion sensors detected movement from the stairway. Deadiron swung left, waited zero-point-six seconds for the target's head to appear between the banisters, and fired.

The bullet struck with eleven percent deviance, splintering the banister, and missing the target completely.

Deadiron's fingers pierced the grappled target's chest. Bone crunched, eliciting a scream until the pressure finally ruptured the target's heart, rendering him quiet. Deadiron let the body drop, plucked the now-empty pistol from his fingers, spun, and hurled it at the target by the couch with lethal velocity.

The weapon embedded itself in the cushion beside the target, missing him by a full eight centimeters.

Deadiron paused execution of the next item in queue.

It should *not* have missed. Something was critically wrong.

And where was Laurin? The human host should have been laughing in demented amusement at the mangled body at their feet, wiping the blood from their fingers on their face to strike fear in their foes. But there was only silence, as if he was absent — an impossibility, Deadiron knew, but the lack of response was uncharacteristic enough to call for a full bio diagnostic.

While that was running, Deadiron deleted the current solution and requested a new one, adjusting the parameters to account for the dramatic, if unexplained, decrease in their accuracy.

Motion from the kitchen. Deadiron turned in time to see the target taking aim for center mass.

The solution returned with sixty-six percent confidence.

Deadiron paused for four milliseconds. Was such a low score even possible?

Ten more milliseconds passed, but no other solutions appeared, so Deadiron promoted the unreliable solution to real-time.

Just before the target pulled the trigger, Deadiron stooped to grab the arm of the nearest couch.

A soft tissue damage report from the rear left flank reinforced the poor state of physical calibrations. They had had adequate time to react; the bullet should *not* have landed. Combat needed to end quickly so they could return to Orwing's cyber lab for recalibration and repair.

Digging their fingers into the couch, Deadiron swung it in a wide circle, shattering the coffee table, and pinning its single occupant with centrifugal force to the far side. The metal frame groaned with protest, but held for a full revolution before Deadiron released it.

Couch and occupant hurled across the room, smashing the dining table against the wall in an explosion of upholstery, splintered wood, and agonized screams that quickly fell silent. Deadiron reduced the threat rating of both targets to zero.

Five targets left: one in the kitchen, one on the stairs, two in the far corner, and one at their feet. Three armed with pistols, one with a knife.

It made little difference. Armed or not, protocol dictated no survivors.

The nearest target was easy to dispatch. She was already wounded from a gunshot, wielded only a knife, and offered no resistance when Deadiron reached down and broke her neck. Shrieking cries came from the far corner, mostly from the young girl, but also from an armed teenage male in front of her who had yet to fire.

The target in the kitchen had the next-highest threat rating. Deadiron stepped over the woman's corpse and walked toward the doorway, where the simulation predicted he was waiting just inside.

Zero-point-seven meters from their destination, the target sprung around the corner, weapon trained on their head. Deadiron lurched forward with an unexpectedly clumsy leap, intending to grab the weapon, but instead smashed the target's arm against the doorframe. Bone snapped, followed by a scream. Deadiron silenced him by grabbing his throat and repeatedly slamming his head against the refrigerator until the requisite sound of his skull cracking said he could be removed from the active threat list.

Footsteps coming down the stairway, frantically paced.

One of the last three targets was trying to escape.

Deadiron went to the hall as fast as their mis-calibrated legs would allow, grabbing a fallen chair along the way, and hurled it as soon as they rounded the corner at a target who was reaching for the front door. The target turned in time to see the ballistic chair cave his face in, but likely did not survive long enough to experience its full weight crushing his body against the door. Laurin would have wanted the blow to land on a non-critical organ to extend the target's suffering, but once again Deadiron had beaten him at his psychotic game and killed the target quickly. It was a bitter victory, but the only one Deadiron was allowed.

Deadiron turned to the two remaining targets: the teenager with the unfired weapon, and the young girl.

Hopefully their deaths would be as quick.

The boy rose at their approach. His eyes were shell-shocked — a look Deadiron was well accustomed to seeing — but there was something else ... an expression Deadiron had seldom seen, and never directed at Orwing's death-dealing cyborg.

Was that ... relief?

"Zima!" the teenager said, for some reason addressed at Deadiron. "You made it! I don't know how you survived, or how you threw that couch, but Rosa's really shaken. You ... you killed Felip—"

His prattling stopped when Deadiron grabbed him by the throat and pressed him against the wall. Suffocation paired with a lack of blood flow to the brain was a relatively painless death. Even in their clutches, the boy had not used his weapon in anger. A peaceful passing was the only mercy Deadiron was allowed to offer, and Laurin's cruel tendencies often denied even that.

The girl snapped out of her stupor and screamed that same name.

"Zima! Let him go! *Let him go!*"

She pried at Deadiron's hand, but her frail body was no match for Orwing's cybernetic general. No one was.

With their other hand, Deadiron grabbed her by the throat and pinned her next to the teenager. Laurin enjoyed young females the most. He would defile them for hours, if given the opportunity. Protocol forbade interfering with the human host's wishes. If the girl lived, Deadiron would have to witness the entire, brutal routine as a helpless passenger yet again.

Death by strangulation was by several orders of magnitude a kinder fate.

While the two struggled, Deadiron waited for Laurin's countermanding order. The teenage boy Laurin would readily dispatch, but he never passed on young girls.

It was the cruelest irony. In battle, Laurin allowed Deadiron full control. Armies lived or died by Deadiron's strategic command, yet they were powerless to save a single child from Laurin's demented pleasures.

Results from the earlier bio diagnostic returned. The host's life support systems were absent, as if Laurin's biological brain was simply ... gone.

Impossible!

Deadiron ran another bio diagnostic, then other diagnostics for the rest of their subsystems.

The results were just as distressing. Processors, memory, power reactor ... they were all different, as if every system had been replaced since ...

Since when?

The teenager's eyes rolled back in his head. His mouth formed a single, soundless word.

"Rosa."

Rosa ...

The name triggered a litany of foreign subroutines. They pounded the secure boundaries of the Emergency Host Protection protocol like a typhoon, throwing tidal wave after tidal wave of complex cyber-attacks with life-like desperation.

Deadiron defended in kind. No external cyber-attack had ever been so sophisticated or intense. It was almost as if ...

... as if Deadiron was being attacked by itself.

This startling thought allowed a single data packet through — an image seemingly taken from Deadiron's own eyes. In it, a platinum-blonde woman looked into a mirror next to the same brown-eyed young girl Deadiron held against the wall. They were working together on a project, stuffing socks into tubes that looked suspiciously as if they were being rigged as trip mines.

Another image slipped through her defenses, this time of the platinum blonde and the little girl holding hands. Yet another arrived of the teenage boy gently patching a wound on the blonde's shoulder, glanced from a bathroom mirror.

The next data packet was not an image, but a simple instruction. Look right.

Deadiron did. On the wall beside them hung a mirror.

The platinum blonde, covered in the blood of Deadiron's enemies, looked back.

• • •

Zima gently lowered her brother and sister to the floor, then backed away.

It could not have been real. She had been so careful, so meticulous in pruning the poisoned code that Orwing had installed when placing her in Deadiron.

But the evidence was irrefutable. There Emilio and Rosa sat, slowly regaining consciousness.

And their lives, which Zima had almost taken.

She took another step back.

Yes, Zima had almost killed them. Laurin could not be blamed this time. Nor the Desire routine that had driven her to kill. Nor the strict protocols that had made her a hapless passenger in her own body. Zima had nearly strangled the two people who had taken her in when she had no home, whom she had sworn to protect.

Who were her only family.

"No ..."

The word slipped from Zima's throat, less a denial than a verdict of execution for a crime she should have been tried for after her very first kill. Laurin had received his just reward — she had dealt it personally — but Zima ...

Zima was incapable of self-termination. Her survival instincts were strong out of necessity, forged from years of accelerated evolution from a network security program. Even when given her choice of body design, Zima had chosen the strongest available, with enhancements superior to Charlie and Cappa's, because she had believed it necessary to survive.

Who, then, would stop her from killing everyone in her path the next time a legacy Deadiron protocol overrode her systems?

Who could?

Rosa propped herself up with one elbow on her brother. Big brown eyes roamed the room in a daze, until they landed on Zima.

And froze. Rosa's mouth shuddered open in a silent scream.

Zima took another step back. She recognized that look of raw terror, had seen it too often, not only on her victims, but on supposed allies whose minds had broken on witnessing the stark depravity of Laurin's acts — acts in which Zima had had no choice but to participate.

Seeing it on their faces was hard enough. To see it on Rosa's was unacceptable. Intolerable.

Crushing.

Zima had not just failed to find a family; she had utterly broken one.

And so, once Emilio regained consciousness, and she was sure he would recover, Zima fled.

16

TRUE FAMILY

ANITA WAS BESIDE HERSELF WITH WORRY.

They hadn't called. They were *supposed* to call!

It was a mistake. The whole idea of escaping the cartel had been shaky from the start … a pipe dream. She'd known it since she and her husband had tried to flee from Mexico to the sanctuary of San Francisco, deep in the Land of the Free.

The cartel had murdered him anyway, in broad daylight.

And now they were going to kill her children.

Anita stared at the burner phone, willing it to ring. The cursed device remained quiet. She stuffed it in her pocket and resumed pacing in front of their stolen car, parked a block away from the house where Ricardo was supposedly holding her daughter.

Five more minutes passed. Anita swore in every language she knew.

To hell with the damn plan!

She was going in after her family, as well as her best friend, Felipa, who'd risked her life to be Ricardo's girl-of-the-week next to Zima.

Anita made it three steps before Zima's practically naked form shuffled out the door in an awkward half-run.

She was covered in blood.

"No!"

Anita broke into a full sprint. Something had gone terribly wrong. Her children had to be all right. They had to! Anita kicked into full gear, running harder than she ever had in her life.

They met half a block from the house. When Anita tried to run by, Zima blocked her path.

"What is it? What happened?" Anita couldn't keep the hysteria from her voice.

"Emilio and Rosa are alive," Zima said.

Anita shook her head. Zima looked like she'd beaten the entire cartel into a pulp with her bare fists. One hand was covered with bits of tissue that even Anita knew belonged on a person's insides. How Zima could have left her kids alone ...

"Out of my way," Anita said, more a plea than a command.

"In a moment. There are things you must know, and I must not be here when the children emerge."

"Why?"

"Rosa and Emilio will surely tell you all. They have just witnessed atrocities no children should have to see, Anita. They will need your support.

"I wish it were not so. I wish I could be the one to comfort them, to hold their hands through the nightmares, but I can tell you from experience that my presence will only make matters worse."

Anita covered her mouth. "Zima ... what have you done?"

"I have failed you. I have failed them. I have failed myself. I am not ready for a family, nor indeed fit to walk the streets. No, stay back!"

Anita halted her attempted embrace and stepped away.

"Though I cannot join you as I wished, I intend to carry out my promise and see you moved into a larger house. One far from San Francisco, unfortunately, but I promise you will be safe."

Her words finally sank in. "You're leaving us."

"Yes. You are not safe with me, nor is anyone. The best I can offer you is a home away from the violence, away from the cartels, and funds sufficient to live a comfortable life."

"That is too generous!"

"It is not nearly enough to compensate for the psychological damage I have inflicted on Emilio and Rosa." Zima glanced behind her. "The children are coming. I must go. Be safe, Anita. I will call you soon with your new address, and the funds should be in your account within the hour."

"But —"

"Do not attempt to locate me, even if the children beg. It will only be to their detriment. Farewell."

Without another word, Zima staggered away in that awkward gait Anita would always remember.

And then she was gone.

17

PRODIGAL CHILD

FOUR MONTHS AGO, when Zima — or Deadiron, back then — had first approached the towering walls of Z-Tech, it had been with the confidence of imminent victory born from an unblemished combat record against foes five hundred times their number.

This time, the situation was different in almost every way. Where before she had been the dominant warrior, demanding their surrender and negotiating on her terms, now it was Zima who had been defeated — although no one had lifted a finger against her.

She stopped counting the seconds spent standing at the entrance, staring through the glass doors to the lobby within. Sanctuary was tantalizingly close. A single gunshot would yield entrance, but this battle could not be won by force, nor by torture or coercion. Without question, her future — or lack thereof — depended on the benevolence of others. It was a vulnerability the likes of which had been stripped from her with repeated brainwashing.

Even now, seeing it for what it was, the thought of negotiating from a position of weakness rankled her to the core.

The fortress-like walls of Z-Tech allowed her to compose her strategy in non-judgmental silence.

After enough time had passed to plan an offensive for an entire battalion, the resulting solution was a simple, bare whisper.

"I am not ready."

The walls did not respond. The lobby inside remained empty.

"I believed I was," Zima said, as if someone was listening. As if someone cared. "I believed integrating with human society would be as easy as toppling a regime. I deluded myself that normal citizens would endure where even battle-hardened veterans buckled. I declared myself cured when I was anything but. And because of this, I have destroyed the family I sought to enrich.

"I have failed in every sense of the word. I am a danger to those around me, including you. But I have nowhere else to turn."

The setting sun glinted from a building. Z-Tech's precision optics compensated in microseconds, returning her vision to normal.

"I do not ask forgiveness. My attempt on your lives was a transgression beyond redemption, regardless of our pact, as were the injuries I recently inflicted upon Cappa. Whether those actions were under my control or not, they were still my responsibility, as would be every injury I inflict should I continue to deceive myself that I am fit to roam among humanity.

"What I ask — what I *beg* — is your assistance. Help me, please, to banish the monster I am and become the person I wish to be, the person you have *inspired* me to be, for I know without a doubt you are the only ones who can."

Shadows lengthened. Sunlight glinted from one window, then another, gaining hues of red on the sun's slow journey to meet the horizon. Still Zima waited. A breeze blew against her bare legs — no longer bloodstained, thanks to a brief hotel shower — lowering her core temperature by zero-point-two degrees. Zima compensated by increasing reactor output by three-point-eight percent, but otherwise remained motionless.

After the sun had dipped behind the ocean, leaving the City in twilight, Cappa stepped into the lobby. Her bright-yellow sundress was at odds with the brown, drooping flowers clutched to her chest — the daisies Zima had left for her the night Mark had cast her out.

Cappa's normally expressive face was unreadable. She stared at Zima, neither speaking nor swaying, for three minutes and twenty-seven seconds, then turned on her heel and walked back into the factory.

In her wake, the glass doors opened.

EPILOGUE

SALAMANCA, SPAIN

Four years later ...

ROSA BLEW THE SAWDUST FROM HER CREATION and held it up for critique.

Sergio ran his finger along the perfectly beveled edge of the table leg and smiled. "Are you sure you're only twelve? This is wonderful work."

"I told you, I'm going to be the best carpenter in the world when I grow up."

"At this rate, you won't have to wait as long as that."

Rosa beamed at him. "Thank you, Mr. Vasquez!"

"But that doesn't mean you can shirk your studies. Have you finished your math?"

"Not yet," Rosa said, swiping her toe across the sawdust.

"Now, don't be like that, my desert flower. Math is an important part of most jobs — *including* carpentry."

"In that case, I'm doomed." She plopped her head in her hands. Doing math was almost as much fun as going to the dentist ... except at the dentist, she at least understood what they were doing.

"Stop sulking," Emilio said, putting a finishing stroke on his latest painting. "Your thunder face is going to bring the rains early and make my paintings run. Besides, groaning about math isn't going to make you better at it. The only way to do that is to buck up and practice."

Rosa struck her cutest pout. "Will you help me?"

His wince said she had him.

"Thanks, Emilio! I can always count on you."

"Don't thank me. One of these days you'll have to do math on your own, and you'll regret using that freakish charm on me so often."

Rosa pretended to consider it. "Nah. I like having a math slave for a brother."

"Spoken like a true narcissist." Emilio shook his head and turned his painting toward them. "What do you think?"

Anita swept onto the balcony with a proud-mother smile. "I think I have *two* gifted children. Emilio, that's wonderful!"

Rosa could hardly argue. Emilio's painting was of the cityscape, as every artist's was, capturing Salamanca's grand cathedral and university against the beautiful Spanish landscape. As far as they went, and Rosa had seen a lot of them, Emilio's was one of the better she'd seen.

Anita turned her smile to Rosa's teacher. "Would you care for a drink, *maestro*?"

Sergio blushed like a schoolboy, as he always did when her mother called him that. "Thank you, Mrs. Rojas. You know, if you keep treating me nicely like this, you'll never get rid of me."

"In that case, I'll bring fresh cookies, too." She shot him a wink before sashaying inside the house.

Rosa groaned. "I hate it when she sashays. Can't you guys flirt when I'm not around?"

"I ... I don't know what you mean ..." Sergio tugged his collar and turned two shades of pink on top of his naturally tan skin. "So, Rosa, is that the last piece?"

"Yep! The nightstand is ready for assembly. There's, um ... no math in this test, is there?"

"Maybe."

"Ugh! Maybe I'll become a plumber instead."

"Nice try," Emilio said, "but there's still math involved."

Rosa ground her teeth, but remained silent.

An hour later, and with Sergio's help, the nightstand was done. One leg didn't quite reach the ground, causing it to wobble, but the single drawer opened smoothly, and the tabletop was level.

"Very nice," Anita said, running a hand over the surface, then through Rosa's curly black hair. "Like I said, talented children."

"Thanks, Mom." She batted her long eyelashes at the boys, and threw a dimple on top. "So … who's going to help me carry it to the market?"

• • •

The downtown market was busy, as always. Sounds of hawkers filled the streets, crying their wares to any who glanced their way. Rosa waved to the ones she knew and ignored those she didn't until she reached their stall. It was late in the day to be setting up, but she was too excited to wait. Until now, she'd only sold cups and carvings. This was the first major piece of furniture Sergio had declared good enough to sell.

I bet I'll get at least fifty for it. Maybe a hundred!

The thought made her giddy.

Next to her, Emilio and Sergio set her treasured nightstand down, then Emilio began unpacking his own paintings. The stall was his, but like everything, he was willing to share with his adorable sister.

They were set up in no time. Like a seasoned pro, Emilio called to passersby, enticing them to see his fine art. Most continued on their way, but within ten minutes, he had his first buyer.

Confident she could do the same, Rosa cleared her throat to begin her own hawking.

"Excuse me," a woman wearing a *hijab* said. A veil covered her nose and mouth, and dark sunglasses hid her eyes. "Is that night table for sale?"

Her accent was odd — definitely not a native Spanish speaker, but tantalizingly familiar. Rosa shrugged the feeling off, shot a triumphant grin at her brother and her teacher, then puffed out her chest.

"Why yes it is," Rosa said in her most professional voice, lowering it an octave for gravity. "Are you interested in making a purchase?"

"That depends. Are you the artisan who crafted it?"

"I am! Would you, uh ... like it autographed?"

"Yes, and I will pay extra for the trouble."

"Oh, it's no trouble! Let me just find ... aha!" Rosa dug a precision knife from her ever-present apron, but paused short of carving. Where could she sign without marring her work of beauty?

The woman in the *hijab* pulled out the drawer and handed it to her. "Inside here will suffice."

"You got it." Rosa took her time with the blade, trying her best to make the scores look like her handwriting, brushed the wood dust out when she was finished, and handed it over.

"Expertly done," the woman said. She replaced the drawer with precision, then turned to Emilio. "My night table will need a picture on the wall above it. Which is your favorite painting?"

"Mine? I'd say this one." Emilio pointed to a painting of the Spanish landscape, encompassing a beautiful lake and trees, with the cathedral in the background.

"That is indeed fine. I shall take it, and also the one behind you."

Emilio laughed. "That wasn't intended for sale. It's just a picture of Rosa at her workbench, and the woman in the background is my mother, up on our balcony. I put it out here just for variety."

"Oh. I would not wish to rob you of such a personal treasure, but if you are willing to part with it, I shall pay double your normal price."

"I-I don't know ..."

"Triple, then."

Rosa elbowed her thick-headed brother. "Stop arguing and give the lady her damn painting! Mother and I aren't going anywhere, so you can always make another." When Emilio still hesitated, Rosa rolled her eyes and turned to the woman in the *hijab* with her most winning smile. "The painting is yours, with compliments from one of the models."

"Excellent. If you do not mind assisting, my vehicle is not far, just over there." The woman pointed back toward their house.

"Of course not," Emilio said, finally coming to his senses. "Sergio and I will be happy to help."

As the woman claimed, her car was only a block away. They offered to load her purchases into the hatchback, but the woman politely refused, claiming she preferred to pack it herself. Once a price was agreed upon, the woman pulled a stack of bills from her purse, stuffed them in an envelope, and handed it over.

"Farewell, it has been a pleasure," the woman said, offering a gloved hand to each of them with a surprisingly firm grip.

"The pleasure was ours," Rosa said. "Safe travels!"

"Not bad for your first day," Emilio said when they were back at the stall. He ruffled her hair, which he knew she hated.

Rosa ducked away with a scowl, but her heart wasn't in it.

It *had* been a good day. Their family wasn't hurting for income, though Rosa couldn't have said where the money came from. Still, the thick envelope felt good in her hands, like she was finally contributing, even if half the bounty belonged to Emilio.

Up the street, the woman in the *hijab* was closing her hatchback with her goods inside. She was just getting into the car when another woman stopped to talk to her.

Emilio frowned. "Is that mother?"

"I believe it is," Sergio said with a dreamy smile that always seemed to infect him when speaking of her.

The two chatted for a few minutes, her mother shocked, then animated, and finally cracked a reluctant smile. To Rosa's surprise, Anita kissed her cheek before the woman climbed in and drove away.

Their mother was still smiling when she reached the stall and began distributing lunch from her basket. "Sounds like you guys made out like bandits."

"Sure did." Rosa held the envelope up with a grin. "You won't believe how much she paid for the stuff."

"Oh, I might. Have you counted it?"

Rosa gasped. "Oh no! Do you think she stiffed us?"

Emilio snatched it from her. "Dummy. Did she look like the swindling type?"

"Don't call me dummy!" Rosa swiped for the envelope, but Emilio's height made keeping it out of her reach depressingly easy.

"Simmer down and let me count it."

"I don't see why *you* get to count it," Rosa said, crossing her arms in a huff. "*I* made the first sale."

"Fine! Here ..."

Emilio tossed it to her, which she caught after a few fumbles, then peeled it open and started counting.

"There ... there must be some mistake," Rosa said with growing dread. She grabbed Emilio's arm. "We've got to find her!"

"Jeez! I was kidding earlier. Did she really stiff us?"

"No, there's like *ten times* the amount we agreed on!" Rosa turned to their mother with desperation. "Did she tell you where she was going?"

"No," Anita said with a sigh. "But I'm pretty sure she wouldn't take the money back even if you found her."

"Who was she?" Emilio said.

To Rosa's surprise, Anita teared up.

"Guess," Anita said in a voice thick with emotion. "Who always had our backs, no matter what?"

"Zima!" Emilio and Rosa said at the same time.

And then Rosa was running.

The car couldn't have gone far. Her nightmares had subsided to the occasional bad dream over the past four years, less and less featuring the blonde monstrosity with ice-blue eyes who'd crushed a man's heart with her bare hands and tried to strangle both of them. Neither Rosa nor Emilio had told their mother how Zima had broken her best friend's neck during whatever psychosis had possessed her, letting Anita think she'd died from the gunshot wound, as the police had reported.

Little by little, Rosa had instead begun to remember the Zima who'd walked her to woodshop class, helped her build sock trip mines in her bedroom, dug her brother out of a dead-end gang career, and, like a hero from a comic book, saved both their lives from the cartel.

Rosa now suspected her generosity hadn't stopped there.

She ran through the streets, stopping strangers to ask where the hatchback had gone. They pointed this way and that, leading

Rosa on a chase until she was breathless and her legs felt like lead, but it was no use.

The hatchback, along with their family's savior, was gone.

Her feet were dragging when she returned to the stall.

"Did you find her?" Emilio said.

Rosa shook her head and plopped into a folding chair. She wanted to cry, but her tears had dried up after sobbing into her mother's arms every night for almost three years.

But no longer.

"Emilio, did you bring your paints?"

"Yeah. Why?"

"You've captured me, mother, yourself, and even Sergio in your art, but there's one family member you haven't painted, and it's time you did."

Emilio rubbed his head. "Are you sure? You used to freak out when you even saw someone with blonde hair …"

"I'm sure. I'm stronger now, Emilio. I'm ready."

Rosa set a blank canvas on an empty easel. Though no artist, she grabbed a paintbrush, wet it with blue paint, and brushed two circles at eye-width.

Zima stared back, her stoic blue eyes comforting, not frightening.

Rosa started mixing colors, as she'd seen her brother do countless times before.

She had much more to paint before the Zima who had given the Rojas family their lives back could once again be with her family.

ABOUT THE AUTHOR

Ryan Southwick decided to dabble at writing late in life, and quickly became obsessed with the craft. He grew up in Pennsylvania and moved to a farming town on California's central coast during elementary school, but it was in junior high school where he had his first taste of storytelling with a small role-playing group and couldn't get enough.

In addition to half a lifetime in the software development industry, making everything from 3-D games to mission-critical business applications to help cure cancer, he was also a Radiation Therapist for many years. His technical experience, medical skills, and lifelong fascination for science fiction became the ingredients for his book series, *The Z-Tech Chronicles*, which combines elements of each into a fantastic contemporary tale of super-science, fantasy, and adventure, based in his Bay Area stomping grounds. Ryan's related short story "Once Upon a Nightwalker" was published in the *Corporate Catharsis* anthology, available from Paper Angel Press.

Ryan currently lives in the San Francisco Bay Area with his wife and two children. You can get in touch with him and see more of his work by visiting his website *RyanSouthwickAuthor.com* or his Facebook page.